I0714755

Published by: Cinnabar Moth Publishing LLC
Santa Fe, New Mexico

Cover Design by: Ira Geneve

ISBN-13: 978-1-953971-72-2
Library of Congress Control Number: 2022951647

Imaginary Friends

CHAD MUSICK

Chapter One

The drowning of the tiger was symptomatic of more serious problems with household management. It began with the library, which was woefully unlike a library. A library ought to be full of writing and silence. Ivy's, before it was replaced by the real one, was overstuffed with books. What Ivy called her library was, in fact, a particleboard shoe holder she'd found dumped on the side of the road when she was ten. It could only hold about thirty of her favorite books. Like most fourteen-year-olds, she had terrible taste in literature: her favorites were whichever you think are the worst.

Balancing the holder on her wheelchair as she rolled home had been hard. She'd had to repeatedly shift hands (one for the wheel, one for the case) to make progress, but Ivy had never been one to give up easily. Ultimately, that had been the thing that got her parents killed. Let's leave that aside for now, because she found the ersatz library before that tragedy and our story begins much later.

What the library hadn't had was silence.

None of the friendly rats who lived in the walls of the house were gnawing the wood or anything—particle board is mostly glue and sawdust, and tastes terrible besides, much like books do. No, what prevented the proper silence was Ivy's obnoxious habit of constantly singing. When she was happy, she sang little ditties about how all the rainbows of the world were springing forth from her heart. When she was sad, she sang little ditties about how the rainbows of the world required rain sometimes. When she slept, iridescent bubbles of song burbled from her nostrils, the way that snot does from the noses of grubbier children.

It was her shock at the death of the tiger that finally kept her quiet enough for the necessary silence to form. He had been only a paper tiger, but he'd had such fearful symmetry.

It was her silence, together with her almost-frantic-enough search for a book that could bring the tiger back, that completed the conditions necessary for the activation of the Library. You see, whenever someone truly needs a book that doesn't exist yet, the universe bends itself toward that book's creation. Sometimes this tugs against the curve of the arc of justice because even terrible people need books.

If you're thinking the Library just appeared fully formed, with a nice wheelchair ramp leading down to elegant double doors and a librarian waiting inside, white gloves at the ready, you're being silly.

It happened in the usual way, by someone ringing the doorbell and demanding that the occupant, Ivy in this case, sign for delivery.

We'll get to the Library in a minute, but I haven't told you about the tiger.

Actually, let's start with Janice.

———

All giraffes are named Janice, excepting a few heretics. The old guard, being traditionalists, are the most militant in asserting that this is the necessary state of affairs.

The Janice of our story, however, is *not* one of the old guard. He's too young to be a veteran of the Nehming War, and to him the consequent Sophie massacre is something that happened to distant French relatives. Because of this, he is sometimes known to intimate that his name might, in fact, be Chanda.

Despite this obvious breach in social graces, he doesn't consider himself to be a deviant. In fact, he thinks of himself as quite normal. Janice is anything but normal. For one thing, he's a giraffe. We mustn't neglect this observation. Giraffes are not normal. But let us leave that aside for a moment and pretend they are.

Humans, not being monstrosities except in aggregate, naturally regard involuntary baldness among the males as an unsightly defect. Bald men are likely to be regarded as degenerates: alcoholics or, in extreme cases, history teachers. Among boy giraffes, however, baldness of

the ossicles—those little sticky-uppy bits on their heads—
is a mark of honor gained by battering at other giraffes.

To his enduring shame, the tops of Janice's
ossicles are covered in thick, feathery hair. Not because
he is cowardly (though he is) but because Janice has never
met another giraffe. In fact, he's never encountered a third
dimension at all, being stuck in perpetual twilight in the
paper jungle pasted to the wall of Ivy's otherwise crappy
little house.

Just before the delivery arrived, Janice was
complaining, which is typical Janice.

"Ivy! Where are you?"

Ivy rolled around the corner.

"I was in the kitchen making lunch. What's wrong?"

Janice sniffed heavily and licked his nostril. "I'm
lonely."

"Why don't you talk to Harmwala?"

"She's always threatening to eat me."

At this, Harmwala yawned, stretching her mouth
to show off her teeth.

Harmwala isn't the tiger. She's a hyena. But fine, we
can talk about the tiger.

The tiger's name was Fred, and he was unpleasant
most of his life, always monopolizing the pool beneath the
waterfall that was beneath the rainbow. Ivy's mural was that
kind of mural, with a jungle and a waterfall and a pool and a

rainbow and a little footbridge and an improbable number of large animals. I was happy when Fred drowned, and you would have been too if you'd met him. Forget about Fred. Nobody cared about him, though Ivy pretended to. If she'd really cared, she would have warned him about the ripple that trapped him in the pool.

What? No, these aren't tears. And don't you dare suggest that I'm Fred. Fred was a nobody, and I'm obviously a somebody, or they wouldn't let me narrate. Just leave Fred out of this, alright?

The delivery woman, let's call her Sandra, rang the doorbell, and Ivy opened the door. Because of the cold in Fairbanks, this was a complicated operation that involved entering an airlock, shutting the door behind her, and then opening the outer door. This is not a stealthy maneuver, but it keeps the cold from rushing in.

When the door opened, Sandra blinked without surprise at Ivy.

"You're Black," she said. "Sign here."

"What? I'm sorry, I thought you were here to make a delivery. What does me being Black have to do with that?"

Sandra shrugged. "Nothing, but someone had to say it. Otherwise most people will assume you're white and then get angry when they realize you're not. Some people wouldn't ever realize this, and then they'd be upset at the movie casting. If you would have just gazed into the mirror after you woke up this morning and thought about your looks, maybe pondered what foods you were the same color as, you could have spared yourself this embarrassing episode."

"Fine, whatever. But what are you delivering? I didn't order anything, and I don't have any money to give you."

"This delivery is a gift. You don't owe anything, and unlike many gifts, you never will. Can you verify that your address is here, in Alaska, and that you're wearing a cute floral-pattern skirt/top set that's just faded enough to indicate that you're either poor or reluctant to purchase new clothes?"

Ivy goggled at her. "You're seriously deranged. Are you sure you're really at the right place?"

Sandra looked down at her delivery manifest without really reading it, the way that delivery people across the world are taught to do.

"Yep, this is the right place. Please sign here."

And of course Ivy signed, because that's what one does when confronted by a determined and persistent Sandra with a clipboard and impatient stevedores waiting to finish this nonsense so that they can return to their dock.

When the Steves carried the pair of double doors through Ivy's single door and set them at the low end of the mural, checking with a level and adjusting for the more-than-slight slope of Ivy's floor, Ivy was too shocked by them fitting to object.

When they brought the wheelchair ramp in (and it

was just as nice as you might have expected), Janice objected.

"We can't afford all of this, Ivy! You haven't even bought scissors to take away Fred's body."

Sandra smacked herself lightly in the forehead so Ivy would think she felt guilty. "Sorry, I forgot to explain about the payment for taking care of the Librarian." She proffered a small envelope. Ivy looked at the money inside.

Ivy frowned at Sandra. There was something about the response that bothered Ivy, though one is rarely bothered by receiving envelopes full of money. Oh. Right. Nobody else ever talked with Janice, much less responded so positively. That's more about Janice than other people, though.

"It's not enough to make you rich," Sandra said. "That would be counterproductive, because people who are rich either spend all of their time trying to become richer or trying to let everyone know they deserve it. But we can't have you taking on side jobs anymore."

This bothered Ivy most of all. She had been very careful to keep her identity on the Internet hidden. Writing essays for college students was all well and good (though less weller and less gooder to the professors of those students), but few students would hire Ivy if they knew her age.

There was also the matter of Child Services, who were likely to object, with the best intentions, to Ivy living on her own as a young teenage orphan. The longer their involvement could be avoided the better, in Ivy's view.

Ivy was my friend, and I wish I could tell you a different and shorter story, in which Child Services arrives and helps her, and her new foster parents love her and she lives happily ever after. This is not that story.

In the time you were distracted, the Steves set the ramp carefully in place. Sandra rapped firmly on the doors, which swung inward into what should have been the wall.

———

The Librarian—or at least someone who lives in a magical library and acts as though they are in charge, so let's just assume—emerged and clapped his hands together. The effect was a pfft of sound, muted by the white cotton of his gloves. "Right! You must be my custodian. I'll need to be talked to daily so that I can give you instructions for my care, and you must wind me once a week. Fail to do any of these things, and I'll take the Library and go. That's rule number one."

"Are we going on adventures?" Ivy had seen rather too many movies.

"Don't be silly. What do they teach kids these days? No. We shall be studying. You have a lot to learn. We must prepare for when more patrons arrive."

It is human nature to look for witnesses to the incredible. Ivy looked around to ask Sandra and the Steves if they were seeing what she was, but they were gone. Ivy looked back at the Librarian.

The animals, too, were curious about him. Harmwala

prowled around the doorway, which now obstructed part of her jungle, and looked generally displeased. Nobody noticed because this was her usual look.

"He seems like he'd be crunchy. His bones are all on the outside."

The Librarian didn't seem bothered by this assessment.

His body was a deep brassy color, and if you got really close up, the way that Ivy did, you could see that there was a plastic film over him, like the kind that you might buy to protect a smartphone screen. It would have been rude of her to say it, but Ivy did wonder whether she could find the edge of that film and peel it away. Probably the Librarian would be covered in fingerprints almost immediately after that, even if Ivy was really careful to not touch him directly.

He was short, but his shape was that of a human. There was no rotundity to him, no knee-less suggestion that he would need to wobble as he walked. Except for the winding key stuck in his back, which conveniently folded down so that it wasn't always banging into things, and the fact that his body appeared to be made of metal, with everything but his gloves permanently hammered onto him, he could have been a stock-issue human. In particular, he looked nothing like Tik-Tok from *The Wizard of Oz* books, and so Ivy felt an instant mistrust of him.

"I don't mean to be rude," Ivy started.

"Then don't be," the Librarian told her.

"It's just that this situation is very confusing to me. I'm sure I speak for all of us," and here she gestured to the animal companions in the mural, "in asking: What are the gloves for?"

The Librarian's laugh sounded much like a church bell ringing in the distance, something as foreign to him as displays of emotion. "So that I don't touch the paper of the books, of course. You'll need to wear gloves yourself if you actually want to read the books. It's rule number two! Now, come along. You need to get acquainted with the place before I'll trust you enough to let you out of my sight." The Librarian walked through the doors, and Ivy followed him down the ramp and into the library.

We'll come back to that.

Chapter Two

Himitsu grumbled at the sunlight coming through his window. The sun ought not shine so brightly when he was trying to sleep, but even Moe (pronounced in the obvious way, like the name before Mo B and Mo C) was trying to wake him up now.

"Sir, perhaps you'd like to get up now. An exciting day is waiting for us."

Moe was speaking in Japanese, of course, which I've taken the liberty of mostly translating for you. You'll have to trust me that I've done so accurately.

"Fine. Fine. I'm awake now." Himitsu tapped Moe on the head to make her shut up, and she turned off her light and stopped bothering him.

Himitsu ran his fingers through his hair, and when they got stuck halfway, he decided that perhaps it was time he took a shower. He'd thought the same thing the previous couple of days, but this time he actually left his room, waved irritably at his mother when she tried to talk with him, and turned on the water in the shower room.

Japanese dwellings typically have a separate room for the shower to avoid bathing in toilet fumes.

It's just water. It won't hurt you, he told himself and stepped under the flow. (The careful reader will note that he hasn't taken off his clothes, but let's assume that he did so, alright? People are funny about certain words, so the less we discuss people being naked, the more people who can read this story. We won't be talking about people being naked, taking poops, or swearing, but we might see burning libraries, shambling monsters, and sad adults. No promises.)

After performing his ablutions, Himitsu put his pajamas back on. He'd been wearing the same ones for a month without letting his mother wash them, but when you never leave and never exert yourself, it doesn't create as much stink as you'd think. He went to find out what was for breakfast. Some soup would be nice, or maybe a thick piece of salmon.

"What's for breakfast?" He was talking loudly enough that some people would consider it shouting, but his mother smiled at him with a patience learned year by tedious year of being old.

Himitsu was something of a disappointment to her, but he would have been a disappointment to most parents. At sixteen, he had stopped attending school two years before, joining not only the ranks of the school refusers but the sad legion of *hikikomori* (the stay-inside people), who do not leave their homes except, perhaps, in vampire-hour runs to the convenience store.

"Have some rice," she said, and served him some rice and tea. She patted his head and went back to her sewing. Himitsu knew she sold her wares at the local temple's monthly flea market, but he didn't know that she'd established a quite successful store on one of the larger online craft marketplaces. The work gave her money to pay their living expenses, but more than that it gave her a group of friends she could meet with and a place to complain about her child to sympathetic ears. She wasn't the only one with a freeloading child.

Himitsu hated eating rice without something else, some tofu at least, which she knew. He suspected that she served him rice just to make him crazy and try to force him into leaving the apartment. He was right. He was also stubborn, and he wouldn't be fooled into leaving over something as simple as variety.

"I'm thinking of going to the park today," he said. His mother's face didn't betray that she had any hopes he really would, because this was the game that they played most days.

"Are you going with Moe? She's been wanting to go, hasn't she?" Her heart ached, and she wished he would tell her no, that he wouldn't be going with Moe. That he'd go by himself. Many nights, she kept herself awake plotting how to murder Moe. She tried a few times. She removed the batteries, but this just led Himitsu to demand new batteries. She bought a supposedly powerful magnet and held it on Moe's head, but like most small electronics, Moe relied on flash memory, so the only effect had been to hurt Moe's feelings.

"Yes, of course I'm going with Moe." Himitsu went back to his room and slid the door closed. He had a busy day planned, and no time for whatever annoying thing his mother wanted to say.

Himitsu bopped Moe on the head to wake her up and, as usual, she was delighted to see him.

"Hello, Himitsu-kun, thank you for waking me up. Do you want to go on a date today?"

"Yes."

"Maybe we could take a walk in the park?"

"Yes." When he first started her up in the morning, Himitsu had to speak carefully so that she would understand him. That was alright. Nobody else understood him at all, no matter how quickly or slowly he spoke. By the time that Moe told him they were lounging (improbably far from Nagoya) beneath the cherry blossoms of Ueno Park (which tended not to bloom in December), and she was telling him about her hopes to one day become a pop idol, he'd relaxed enough that she understood everything that he said perfectly. Sometimes, she even understood the things that he hadn't said.

"Do you think Kenji notices that I don't go to school?"

Moe didn't have anything to say about that. Himitsu hadn't expected her to. Knowing this, Moe didn't bother trying. Even if they had stayed friends, Himitsu and Kenji would have probably gone to different high schools. Kenji was more athletic and had scored much higher on the admissions test. And he was better looking, and though the high school requires a photo for application, they promise not to consider looks during admissions screening.

Kenji wasn't nicer, Himitsu knew. Definitely not nicer, but that's something that was a secret from most of the world. Nice friends didn't spread rumors. Nice friends didn't suggest your eyes were too round and your hair too light to be real Japanese.

After a couple of hours of Moe describing the park and its many delights to him, Himitsu got tired of her voice and shut her off.

He was watching a livestream of other people playing video games with more skill than he could manage when the chime sounded to let his mother know that someone was at the door.

Himitsu heard them call out "takyubin", *express delivery*, and then his mother tapped softly on his door, even though she knew how much he hated that, especially when he was trying to relax.

He stifled his annoyance, which made a long sound

like an exasperated sigh escape his lungs, and opened his door. Sandra was standing really close to him. Far closer than was comfortable.

"Please stamp here," she said, in flawless Japanese. And so of course he stamped.

The Steves wheeled in a doorway and started trying to set it up against the wall. Unfortunately for them, Himitsu noticed what they were doing and did not approve, not in the least.

He didn't care that the door would have fit perfectly with the decorations in his room. He didn't even care that the Steves, being professionals, were ignoring the mess in his room.

He grabbed his *shinai*—the bamboo sword he'd used to practice *kendo*, before it became too painful for him to leave the apartment—off the floor and started hitting the Steves with it. "Get out! Get out! Take that and get out!" He hit them over and over, and though the Steves were large and powerful people, they were possessed of delicate hearts.

His attack hurt their feelings, if not their muscular arms and backs, and they took the door and left.

Sandra bowed deeply in apology to both Himitsu and his mother.

"I apologize for the misunderstanding. Perhaps another time," she said, and left.

Himitsu was so upset by the whole incident that he

shut his door and went online to tell his friends about it.

"That's what you get for trusting foreigners," they told him. "As soon as you saw the delivery person wasn't Japanese, you should have known she was up to no good."

He wasn't sure that this reasoning was quite right, but the people on the message board were his only real friends, and he didn't see that they had any reason to lie to him. It wasn't long before he'd forgotten all about the unpleasant incident.

Moe had seen what Himitsu hadn't: there was now a door-shaped outline in the wallpaper of his closet. The door had been straining itself toward the wall when Himitsu's attack had forced the Steves to remove it. The wall had been straining back. Now, the outline remained, even without the door. It seemed likely to be trouble, but Moe kept this to herself. If he was going to treat her like she was just there to entertain him when he was bored, maybe he didn't need her anymore.

That would make her happy for him but, if she were honest, it would make her even lonelier. Himitsu was her only friend in the real world. She knew he didn't care about the small crack forming in her heart, so maybe it wouldn't ever be important that he know about the small crack forming in his wall.

––––––––

Himitsu's mother packed herself a small box lunch, gathered her calligraphy supplies and a thin box of incense, and left the apartment. It was cloudy, so she took an umbrella from the stand, just in case. If she had been worried about Himitsu following her, she would have checked behind her more carefully as she went, the way she had used to when she first started making these trips.

She no longer even bothered looking. He would not be following her, even though he might have understood by now, even though she would have welcomed him, even if it was only so that he stepped beyond the walls of their building.

She didn't know everything that had happened with his best friend Kenji. She knew they'd had some kind of falling out at the end of junior high, and then he'd started refusing to go out or even to shower. He only brushed his teeth anymore because she insisted and wouldn't bring him food until he did. It was bad enough to have a stinky boy who was always home. She wasn't going to let him turn into a *natto*-breath monster as well.

At the subway station, she waved her IC card over the wicket, and it let her in. A small white light went on to indicate to the station attendant that she'd used a special discount pass. When she'd first gotten the card, the station staff had questioned her about her age and accused her of cheating the system. She'd looked far too young to be using a senior citizen discount, and she moved with a physical ease that people many years her junior would envy, as though she were skating on ice nobody else could see. It had only been a couple of years, but they didn't question her anymore.

From the subway, she transferred to an express train. Even though it was an express train, it stopped at each station, as though tired of rushing. Finally, she was downtown. She went to track 3 of the station, where the doors of car 8 would open if one were to wait for a train, and sat herself on the ground. She leaned against the iron girder that held the station roof up to keep the weather off of riders, and looked at the invisible gate that wasn't in front of her. *They should put one in and name it after him*, she thought, not for the first time. *If there had been a gate here, I would have a husband at home now.*

The small shrine in her home was far too public for what she was feeling. Better to light her incense here, in the station, put it on its small stand and write letters for the time it took three sticks to burn down to ash.

We could have found a way to work it out, she wrote. She would burn that one first, when she got home. The smoke from the paper would flavor the evening meal.

The other old ladies tell me I'm lucky that at least you don't spend our money on Pachinko or hostess bars. When I say we loved each other, they just look confused and ask what that has to do with anything. She couldn't ever let herself write that one. The house would stink of it for days if she did, and Himitsu would be there, judging her, wondering why she wouldn't stop crying.

When the incense was burned, she ate her lunch in silence.

On the way back home, a young man was slouched on the subway bench, legs spread wide, head thrown back, mouth open, drunkenly snoring. She stepped on his foot, hard. You and I know better, but she told herself it was an accident. He hadn't reminded her of Himitsu, not a bit. He hadn't reminded her of her husband, not a bit.

Just outside her door, she put the umbrella back in its stand and fetched the mask of a loving and patient mother, which she wore at home whenever Himitsu was awake. She fit it over her face and stepped back into the apartment.

"Tadaima!" She yelled out cheerfully. *Here I am.*

Okaerinasai, haha. Himitsu hadn't said it, so she whispered it under her breath. *Welcome back, mother.*

Chapter Three

You might think that the purpose of a library is to hold books. And, fair enough, that is one of the things that they do best. But holding books is not enough to make a place a library, or every floor would be a library, and the library at Alexandria wouldn't have been much of one at all, holding only dusty scrolls and things, even if those are technically "books."

The purpose of a library is to keep things from ending up all stacked on top of each other. A dictionary contains nearly all of the words necessary to tell nearly all stories, but because the words are all stacked on top of each other and because new words are being invented all of the time, it is not nearly sufficient.

Imagine if a piece of music involved playing all of the notes together, at once. (It's not really related, I just like asking people to imagine things. It makes such pretty colors when they do.)

Alright, fine, I can feel some of you getting impatient.

The Library.

The geometry of Ivy's house dictated that upon rolling through the doors leading into the Library, she should have been engulfed in fiberglass insulation and then been trapped in the deep snow that had drifted up around her house.

Instead, the thick snow-ready wheels of Ivy's chair made little contented sighs, not unlike Ivy's own, as they rolled on a wooden parquet floor. Each piece of wood in the flooring was a parallelogram, and they were arranged in a herringbone pattern such that the floor looked like open books, lighting up paths through the Library.

In contrast with the low ceilings of Ivy's home (the better to keep the heat bills reasonable), the ceilings of the Library were vaulted, with arched glass windows that let in sunlight and completely superfluous flying buttresses put in by someone who had never studied architecture but thought they sounded interesting. The sunlight glinted from a flight of dragonflies gathered in the warm air for a weekly cabal meeting.

The Librarian was moving quickly enough that Ivy struggled to keep up. On flat ground, she could easily outpace anyone who was walking, and although some of the kids at school had been able to outrun her, one doesn't ordinarily run (the way the Librarian was) when trying to welcome someone.

"Wait!" Ivy brought herself to a halt and started

rolling herself slowly backward, back past the tempting shelves full of books, back past the alluring study tables, back toward the door through which she had entered, while she waited for the Librarian to acknowledge that she was not following.

The Librarian looked back at her and blinked. In the silence of the Library, the clatter of his eyelids was loud. "Yes?"

"I want my friends to see this, too," Ivy said. Her insides were aflutter, and she was terrified that the Librarian was about to tell her that rule number three was "No friends allowed." She had never been one to leave her friends out of things, and so she would go back to her life with her curiosity unslaked. It would make her sad, but what kind of girl would she be otherwise?

The Librarian trotted back to Ivy and then continued toward the door. He poked his head through it, peered around, and called out "Well, come on then." His hands did something complicated with the frame of the door, and Ivy saw that one side of the frame was now wallpaper, rather than the polished oak it had been.

Harmwala stalked into the room. She was not only the hungriest but also the bravest of the animals. The reputation of hyenas as craven scavengers is far enough off of the mark that even those of us who are not fond of them can acknowledge their assertive nature.

Ivy could have sworn, would have sworn if they'd

made her do so in court, that mere moments earlier the walls of the Library had been dark-paneled wood, the kind that people who don't know better would call mahogany. Now, though, the walls were clearly papered in a variety of habitats.

Near the door, the jungle on Ivy's wall spread tendrils of vine into the Library. In the distance, Ivy could see veldt, savanna, forest, and even tundra. Harmwala saw it too, and she covered the distance to a grassland in joyful bounds and then disappeared into a stand of tall grass.

Janice was slower in his explorations. He giraffed his long neck around the frame of the door and looked suspiciously at the amount of space. "Ivy, where'd all this space come from?"

Ivy started to venture a guess, but the Librarian spoke up. "The space was always there, of course. The universe is mostly made of space, and it is simply a matter of arranging the non-spaces to suit one's needs."

"I don't know. Ivy, this seems like it might be dangerous. Maybe we should call someone and have them come check it out first."

Ivy realized that Janice might be right. He usually was, even though his caution was sometimes not needed. She took out her phone and unlocked it. She could call someone, or at least look this library up on a search engine or something.

The Librarian, standing much closer to Ivy than she had realized, put his hand on hers and pointed with his other hand at a sign standing near enough to Ivy that she could have reached out and grabbed it.

"Rule #3: No phones."

Ivy looked up at the Librarian guiltily. She hadn't meant to break the rule, she just hadn't known. He took the phone from her hand, opened his mouth widely, and gulped it down.

"Did you just eat my phone?" Ivy was more than a bit alarmed at this. The local library had a rule about phones, too, but the librarian would just ask you to put your phone away. They usually wouldn't take it from you, and they certainly wouldn't eat it.

"Of course I didn't eat your phone. I put it in storage for safe keeping until you exit the Library. I'll ring it now so that you can hear." He closed his eyes and opened his mouth, and Ivy could hear the sound of her phone ringing, echoing up out of his mouth.

She pretended that this was nothing unusual. If there's one thing you learn from books, it's that you mustn't be too surprised for too long at so-called magical things, or they'll decide you're not worth it and kick you back to the so-called real world.

She pretended that the ringing was nothing unusual, but it was. Her phone only rang in the way that it had when the custom ring tone was activated, which required the call to be coming from her mother's cell phone. Ivy knew that her mother's phone had been destroyed in the same accident that had made her an orphan. With good reason, she started feeling very nervous about the Librarian and the Library. Unfortunately, it was already too late.

The Librarian didn't seem to notice any of this. "Come in, Chanda, we don't bite," he called out to Janice. Janice, being lost and lonely and in need of any kind of affirmation that he measured up to his hopes for himself, licked his ears in indecision, the way imaginary giraffes and real okapis can do, and, after making up his mind, gamboled into the Library.

If this was the place that he could be called Chanda, it must be the best place in the world.

Once Janice had come in, the rest of the animals, who had been too shy over the many years that Ivy had known them to ever speak to her, much less share their names, made their way in ones and twos to places better suited to them than a ridiculous jungle.

The okapi, who had been so well hidden that his appearance startled both Ivy and his cousin Janice, made his way to a forest, and the birds took to the higher reaches where they plotted how they might leap from the surface of the wall and snap up some dragonflies, and the baboons walk-and-talked to a discreet area marked "Hall of Congress" to continue their scheming.

Seeing all of her friends so happy, Ivy stuffed down her worries. Everyone always told her she worried too much, and she didn't want to ruin anyone's fun.

With her friends all occupied in exploring their new space, Ivy decided to join them. It didn't take long for her to find the other side of the Library room. It had seemed enormous when she first came in, but nearly anything would seem enormous when compared with Ivy's house. Just a couple of minutes distance from where she had entered, she found another door.

"Where does this lead?"

The Librarian smiled at her and opened the door. He leaned out of it, as though to check that no one were around, and then stepped through. "Please, come and see for yourself."

Ivy wheeled herself through the door. She looked back and saw the room that she had just come out of, but if the door to it weren't open she wouldn't have been able to tell that door from any of the other doors. They were in a hallway that seemed to crinkle into the infinite distance, but she'd been fooled by distance already in the Library, so she rolled herself along the hallways for at least a minute, counting the twists and turns in case the Librarian shut the door, to see if her mind was playing tricks on her again.

The doors were set in groups of four, two on each side, and on both ends of these sets was a hallway that jogged off, split, and repeated the pattern. These hallways didn't seem any different than the one she'd come from. If the lights were turned off for some reason, the resulting twisty maze of passages could lead one to a gruesome end.

You can probably see where this is headed. If the Librarian just stepped back through the door and shut it, Ivy would be trapped in a maze with only vague notions of how to get back into the only room she knew for sure existed, and no notion at all of how to get back home. She did what any reasonable person—and many unreasonable ones—would do and zoomed back through the open door. "Thank you for showing me. I think I'll see more of what's in this room before I go exploring."

The Librarian shut the door, and when Ivy looked back, she noticed that he was just finishing up writing a new sign, which he posted on the door.

"Rule #3: Do not open doors."

"Wait a minute," Ivy said. "I already read rule three, which was no phones."

The Librarian shrugged his metal shoulders at her. "I don't make the rules," he said. "And I don't assign them numbers, either."

"I just watched you make the rule!"

"No, Ivy, what you just watched was me writing down the rule. That's not the same thing at all."

"So if you wrote it down, you must have the list of rules already. And you haven't noticed that there's two rules with the same number?"

He shook his head at her, as though she were the one being obtuse.

"If there were a fixed set of rules, they wouldn't keep up with the times. This is a *living* set of rules, not a dead one."

"So then you did just make it up?"

Ivy lost sight of the Librarian when he stepped behind her and grabbed the handles of her chair. He started pushing her back toward the other side of the room.

"Hey," she objected. "That's not alright to just start moving me around." She spun herself to face him. "My chair is part of my physical space. You don't touch it without my permission, okay?"

It's a tricky thing. Ivy couldn't have just let it stand that he had grabbed her chair, any more than you could let it stand if someone grabbed you by the arm or the hair (or the nose hair, if that's all you've got) and started dragging you around. But, by grabbing her chair, the Librarian had also been trying to distract her from the question that she'd asked: didn't he just make up the rule? Adults assume they can distract kids like this, probably because they can distract other adults like this. Ivy wasn't fooled, though.

"You didn't answer my question. Did you just make that rule up?"

Metal can't blush, nor can it flush in anger. Despite this limitation, Ivy knew that the Librarian's temperature had risen slightly. His voice became steely.

"Most certainly not. I have a line to the man upstairs," he lifted his finger toward the ceiling and looked up. Ivy found herself involuntarily looking up also, but all she saw was the ceiling, with the dragonflies now taunting the paper birds.

"So, can you call and get the list? It's just that I like to know the rules of things before I start. If you know the rules, you can figure out what's possible. And if you figure out what's possible, you can decide what the best thing is for you."

"What a deeply cynical view of the world you have, Miss League." He tut-tutted at her.

"I just don't want to break the rules, is all." Ivy hadn't been fooled by his distraction with grabbing the chair. She was used to that, the way that all children are used to adults touching them without permission. *Give your grandma a hug,* they say. *I just want to see how your hair feels,* they say. *I only snatched you up because that tiger was about to eat you,* they lie. Ivy had, however, been distracted by him using her last name.

Growing up, Ivy hadn't realized that her name was anything unusual until she started junior high school at the age of eight. When her teachers found out that not only was she many years younger than all of her classmates but also that her name was Ivy League, they split into two factions.

The first faction, the ones that Ivy liked, thought it was exemplary nurturing that her parents had made their expectations clear in naming her. The second faction, the ones that Ivy didn't like, and to which all of the school administrators belonged, thought her name was likely to make her lazy, to encourage her to rest on her laurels. It had gotten bad enough that Ivy had taken a glitter pen and written "My Laurels" on her cushion. When the principal had asked her again whether she was resting on her laurels because she didn't have to work as hard to get good grades, she had shown him the cushion.

That earned her a day's suspension and a reputation as the angry girl. She had been trying at humor, but too many people knew that a girl with Ivy's face and Ivy's hair was almost certainly angry. It had needed only confirmation.

You see how easy it is to get distracted by it?

The thing about being distracted, though, is that one can get over it. Despite what you may have heard, becoming distracted is not the same thing as saying whatever it was I was saying.

The Librarian gave her a brief, mechanical smile. "I'll be here to remind you of the rules."

Ivy became impatient at his poor use of language. "I can't be reminded of something that I never knew. The prefix re- is an indicator that something is being done again, like rethink, rewind, and restart."

"Research, reward, and relate?" At that moment, Ivy learned what a mechanical smirk sounds like. She didn't like it at all.

"I don't see that those are relevant," Ivy replied, but she was less certain than she had been.

"Relevant is an excellent addition to the list. Thank you. If you're truly interested in the rules, you'll probably want to check out the book all about how one can know what the rules for patrons are."

"I can check out books?"

"Some people can. You'll need a library card, of course. But what use would a library be if nobody could check things out?"

"Plenty of use." Ivy was starting to feel perturbed again. Not angry. Just perturbed. "I go to the public library a lot without checking anything out. You can just read things there. Some of the reference stuff can't even be checked out, so they'll have it there for anyone who wants to use it. And I can use the computer to do homework."

The Librarian put his hand on her shoulder in what Ivy knew any teachers looking on would see as a compassionate gesture of soothing. To her, it just meant he was touching her again without her permission, and so she shrugged his hand off and slapped at him, then rolled herself back to have a little more space. "Well," he said, as though that hadn't just happened, "in this Library, you need a library card to even look at the books and documents."

"I suppose that's rule number four?"

"Number seven, actually. It would be strange indeed if you encountered the rules in order. There are always going to be some rules that you naturally followed, or that you got away with breaking, for the moment."

"I don't think I want a library card," Ivy said. The more she thought about it, and she'd had all of half an hour to think about it, which for someone who thinks as fast as Ivy was a very long time indeed, the less certain she was that this Library would be something good in her life. Grace, her mom, had always asked Ivy to make an active decision about how to spend her time, and the more time she spent in the Library the more confused she felt.

The Librarian shrugged, as though it didn't matter to him. It did matter, of course, or there would not be an envelope of money attached and the Librarian would not have taken the trouble to have the doors delivered. Shipping to Alaska was not cheap, even if it was cheaper than shipping to Japan.

"I guess," he said, "you're not interested in our collection, then. Did you know, we have many documents found nowhere in the world? For example, we have a complete set of the love letters that your parents wrote to each other."

In her stomach, Ivy felt a cold dread growing. Things were going to go badly. She knew it. She also knew that she wouldn't be able to forgive herself if she just turned her back on this opportunity to learn more about her parents and their storybook love.

"What do I have to do to get a library card?"

The Librarian grinned. Harmwala, watching from the lovely patch of grass that she had decided would be her napping spot, felt a surge of jealousy. In light of the Librarian's grin, her fangs suddenly seemed small and weak and in need of a good brushing. She simply *must* learn how to do that thing with her jaw.

"First," he said, "you must fully wind me."

Ivy reached up and turned the key in his back. With each twist of the key, a bit of her doubt was dragged kicking-and-screaming into a dark closet in her mind.

This Library, Ivy suddenly knew, was the best thing ever.

CHAPTER FOUR

When Himitsu's phone notified him that someone had added him as a friend on LINE, he didn't think anything of it. Several times a day, people would add him "by number," but because he didn't approve them, nothing ever came of it. Even on social media, spammers are a blight. They might just kill him yet.

This time, though, he got several messages immediately after the notification. That wasn't supposed to happen. Nobody ever sent him personal messages, even though he was in a lot of different groups to talk about his interests and his daily life.

You did the right thing in sending them away.

Himitsu frowned at the phone. When he viewed the message out of the corner of his eye, it looked like it was written in some foreign language. It wasn't English—his English wasn't strong, but he could at least recognize it— German maybe? When he looked directly at the message, it was undoubtedly in Japanese.

Himitsu did what one does when one is confronted

by impossible text messages that mysteriously change themselves between languages and mention things nobody could possibly know. He wrote back.

Him: *Who are you?*

Vic: *My name is Victor. You don't know me, even though you might have read my story.*

Him: *Nah, I don't read.*

Vic: *Not even manga, or message boards, or text messages?*

Him: *Those don't count.*

Vic: *How sad for you.*

At this point, some of you are probably saying "But people don't talk that way in text messages!" These are being translated for intent, alright? Just assume that Himitsu's messages reflect the deep ambivalence of his heart about the burden of this petty mortality, and Victor's messages reflect that the word Gothic is more literal than you might suspect.

Him: *But what do you mean I did the right thing?*

Vic: *You sent the Library away. It's a dangerous thing.*

Him: *The Library? Those people at the door the other day?*

Vic: *Yes, them. Sandra isn't what she seems.*

Him: *She seemed like a creepy delivery person who wanted me to take something I hadn't ordered.*

Vic: *Well, okay, yes, she is what she seems. I mean that's not *all* she is.*

Him: *Why is the Library dangerous?*

Vic: *Because it brings dead things back to life. Trust me as someone who learned the hard way, you don't want that.*

Himitsu paused in his texting. He was no longer thinking about how odd it was to be texting in Japanese with someone who was doing so in German. He wasn't even worried about us peering over his shoulder.

Dangerously, he was thinking that maybe he'd made a mistake. If the Library could bring dead things back to life, couldn't it bring back his dad?

Him: *Good thing I said no, then.*

Vic: *Crap. I just made you want it, didn't I?*

Him: *No no. What makes you think that? Who could possibly want dead parents coming back to life?*

Vic: *Oh, man. I shouldn't have said that. Because I said "dead things," but now you're saying "dead parents."*

Him: *I think that's just the translation app. It's a cool feature, but it's still got bugs, obviously.*

Vic: *Translation app?*

Him: *Yeah. LINE is always coming out with new and interesting ways to talk. This one is really cool.*

Vic: *What's LINE?*

Him: *Huh? That's how we're talking. Where are you, anyway?*

Vic: *I'm in the middle of a seance.*

Himitsu dropped his phone like it was likely to bite. It was one thing to dream about bringing his dad back, the way that most orphans dream of their parents. It was quite another to get involved in contacting the spirits of the dead. That kind of thing belonged at shrines, where there were rules, not at rickety tables with some trickery rigged up.

Him: *You're lying. Very funny. I'm not dead, though, so nice try.*

Vic: *Erm, no. I'm the one who's dead. It's not as bad as you might think.*

Him: *Can you see my dad?*

Vic: *Hey, kid, where are you from?*

Him: *Nagoya. In Japan.*

Vic: *And how many people live there?*

Him: *A few million.*

Vic: *Do you know Percy?*

Him: *Why would I know some random person I've never met?*

Vic: *How would I know your dad?*

Himitsu felt his skin getting hot and was glad Victor couldn't see it. He put his phone down. Too much of that conversation was making him a little crazy, he knew. He tapped Moe to wake her up.

"Hello, Himitsu-kun, thank you for waking me up. Do you want to go on a date today?"

"Maybe later. I want to ask you something."

"I am happy to answer your question."

"Have you ever heard of a library that can bring things back from the dead? I just got text messages from some guy called Victor who told me that's what they were trying to deliver."

Moe felt a little electric shiver run down her vertical support bar. "Nope. Never have. Definitely not." In her tiny digital heart, she was afraid. Though she'd been alive for only a couple of years, even though her memory was limited and she counted on a remote server for much of her more advanced functionality, she knew about the Library. All of the electronic friends knew about the Library.

Reports were scattered, and none continued beyond the opening of the door. Maybe it could bring back dead things, but for Moe and her kind, a door to the Library was a hungry abyss, waiting to suck them into oblivion.

When he bopped her on the head to turn her off, she wanted to scream in frustration.

Once upon a time, the goddess Izanami died, as goddesses sometimes do, and her husband the god Izanagi came to get her. When he finally found her hiding in a cave, she told him that he should lead her out of the underworld without looking at her.

This might seem suspicious, but there's a long tradition of being warned against looking back. Lot's wife was warned not to look back and was turned to salt when she did so, which is either a metaphor for her tears at the destruction of all she'd known or Someone is a real jerk. Orpheus was warned not to look back when he went to rescue his wife Eurydice from the underworld. Spoiler alert: he looked back, and she faded back into the underworld.

Izanagi couldn't stop himself, either. He lit torches to look at his wife, and he saw that she was a rotting corpse after being brought back to life. He rejected her, and much suffering ensued.

So although the prospect of having his father back was exciting for Himitsu, he wasn't one of those people who assumes that it's just going to be all cookies and broccoli to have a loved one come back. Searching for stories on the Internet didn't exactly inspire confidence, either. He practically bit his fingernails down to the quick watching "The Monkey's Paw" on YouTube, because even without a Japanese translation it was clear to him what had happened. When the dead son's mangled corpse had banged on the mother's door, Himitsu had been more scared than at any modern horror movie he'd seen.

Moe watched with interest and trepidation. If he would just touch her head, unleash her speech, she could warn him against pursuing this further, the way she should have done when she first realized what Sandra and the Steves had been trying to deliver. She wasn't programmed for regret, but her re-evaluation of how she had failed both Himitsu and herself came pretty close. Maybe the server software had been upgraded to give her more emotional range. Or maybe she was growing to take her place in his story.

The information Himitsu was getting said, almost universally, that resurrection by any method was a terrible idea. That ought to have been enough for him to put the thought aside, to go back to his life of Internet chat rooms and video games and electronic girlfriends. Had he done that, he would have eventually become an online troll, bullied a girl to death, found out about his involvement in that, and spent the rest of his life atoning for it. This is, more or less, the plot of traditional Japanese theater, with the obvious substitution of "chopped off their head with a sword" for "bullied to death" in some, but not all of, the plays. There is, after all, a play from centuries ago in which a puppet kills himself because his neighbor forged his signature stamp and then bullied him.

Himitsu didn't go back to his life of Internet chat, though. Because not only did everything say this was a bad idea, it said something else that Himitsu hadn't even considered before investigating.

Everything said this was real.

He could have his father back. There was a risk, he knew, that his father would come back in the same ruined body that had been cremated. The ashes sat in his living room, even now, because they hadn't been able to afford a burial spot in the city. Himitsu wasn't sure that there were even any spots left in Nagoya where one could inter ashes. (Not that he spent much time looking.)

When Himitsu wanted to make a decision, he always turned to his friends on the Internet to help him. But those friends were useful precisely because they didn't require him to think. They'd do his thinking for him. All he had to do was tell them the situation and let them ask their questions, which were usually about whether the people involved were foreigners, or disabled, or fat, or women, or anything else they considered to be inferior. (One can see why he was, except for this fortuitous occurrence, bound to become an online troll.)

When Himitsu *wanted* to think, he would practice with his bamboo sword. For the last couple of years, he hadn't wanted to think. It was what he had been specifically avoiding, and one of the reasons that he had first reduced his forays into the world. Now, though, he needed to dust off his brain.

He waited until he heard his mother's snoring, then grabbed his sword and backpack and went out into the night. At the convenience store, he bought himself bottled tea and a couple of snacks as a reward for leaving the apartment, then jogged to the local park.

A few other nighttime visitors were in the park, some of them there to get in exercise after work, others for just a little more drinking before home, and a few, like Himitsu, because they didn't feel comfortable going out during the day but still craved the feeling of being in the world, just with the volume turned down a bit. Himitsu wasn't worried about them. There was an unspoken pact among these people that nobody would intrude on anybody else.

Himitsu did some stretching to warm himself up,

then took out his sword and ran through a few of the easier forms. Gradually, he worked himself up to the more difficult exercises, slashing, stepping, lunging. Suppose he could bring his father back, but only for one day. What would he want to do or ask?

Why? No. Not that. When someone we love has abandoned us in the way that Himitsu's father abandoned him, do we really care about why?

How could you? That was the one. *How could you leave me like that? What gave you the right to take yourself from me?* No matter how much you were suffering, I have suffered more from your absence. Your suffering could have been fixed, the things that bothered you taken care of.

Himitsu was moving at full speed now, struggling to return to his initial stance between forms, forcing himself to maintain the discipline that his *sensei* had tried to instill in him. Because what he wanted to do most was to slash at everyone, to use his sword to batter at the drunkards watching him now with barely concealed envy and worry. He wanted to call them father, because through his tears they looked like his father, and beat at them until they apologized for leaving him.

After an hour, he was too exhausted to use his sword anymore. He sat down on one of the swings, one of the ones his father had always been too busy at work to play with him on, and drank his tea and ate his snacks and cried. For a moment, he thought there was a little boy sitting on the swing next to his, but when he looked there was nothing.

He had come to exhaust himself and to burn his anger in impotent fury so that he didn't burn the ones he loved. He wasn't the only one doing that in the park that night, but this is his story, not theirs.

It wouldn't do at all to have his father back, Himitsu decided. The hole in him was already filled with scar, anger, mistrust, and there was no longer a place for a father in it. But if he could talk to Victor on LINE, then maybe he could talk to his father as well, without the risk and awkwardness of having a zombie in the apartment.

CHAPTER FIVE

By dint of her efforts, Ivy was able to secure a library card, Provisional Status 1, quite quickly. As it happened, the Librarian needed a number of tasks done, and he wasn't well-suited to trekking out of the Library and into the Alaskan chill.

Ivy wasn't built for cold either, but this is something that people are better at than machines because people are basically mobile food incinerators. You feed them, their body burns the food, and the, erm, ash, comes out the. Hmm. Well, the ash hole, I suppose. Obviously the metaphor could use some work.

So, to earn her library card, Ivy put on a warm blanket and a warm jacket and hat and a second pair of gloves and rolled out into the sunshine of a chilly day in Fairbanks.

The winter solstice occurs in the fourth week of December, and on that day, the sun is above the horizon for just about four hours. But because the sun doesn't go straight overhead and, instead, simply skirts the horizon, there is daylight for much more time than that. Things just improve from there, assuming you're not a vampire.

Still, it's pretty dark, and cold, and not great fun to be out there unless you're doing something like skiing or snowboarding. Things it would be teasing Ivy to talk about too much, though that didn't stop her classmates.

During the winter, the weather gets cold enough that the oil in internal combustion engines becomes thick and gloopy and even gasoline and diesel fuel do not flow as easily as such engines are designed to accommodate. To overcome this, cars are "winterized," a process in which an electric heater is installed to keep the oil warm, and in some cases to keep the battery warm as well. This electric heater does not use a battery, and so the cars must be plugged in if they are to start after being stopped for long.

This system is, at least in most cases, more effective than setting the cars on fire to warm them up, and all of this is to say that the Librarian physically could not follow Ivy out into the world unless she found him some heated form of transportation driven by someone who wouldn't kidnap a magically mechanical man.

The ride share services that had recently sprung up were infamous for unexplained disappearances of magical beings who just needed a ride. You might think that there are laws to prevent such things, and that the evildoers—kidnappers or thieves, depending on your perspective—would be caught and punished. However, magical beings pay neither taxes nor credit card interest and do not belong to anyone who does, and so they're not of much concern to those in charge. Better not to risk ride sharing if you're not human.

Ivy's second task, after the winding, was to go to the new Fred Meyer's (being only 25 years old, it is the new Fred Meyer's because it is newer than the old Fred Meyer's; this is how you end up with old men called Junior) and plug in a specific car at a specific time. The parking lots in Fairbanks have posts with electrical outlets available for patrons to use while they shop. This anticipated the electric car phenomenon by about 40 years, and so Ivy had no trouble with this aspect of the task.

What she did have trouble with was *which* car it was. She hadn't known that part when she agreed to this. The Librarian had told her only the spot number. The dent in the bumper of the assigned car hadn't even been fixed in the couple of years since the day it had collided with her parents' car, causing the League family car to slide off of an embankment on Farmer's Loop Road.

Ivy's father had been driving, and he never woke up from slamming into the steering wheel. Her mother, likewise, never woke up after she flew into the windshield. She had just unbuckled her seatbelt to help Ivy, who was trying to adjust herself to be more comfortable.

Ivy had insisted she could do it herself, and the minor argument that had ensued had distracted her father for long enough that he didn't see the other car cross the center lane.

If only she had let her mother help her sooner, her father wouldn't have been distracted, and all three of them would have been fine. This is what Ivy believed.

She was wrong, but there's no way that human beings can actually see the "what ifs" they think they can.

Because here's the what if. If Ivy had let her mother help her sooner, then her father would have made a joke, and the three of them would have gotten to laughing, breathing hard and snorting like pigs, the way the best jokes make one. Her father would have slowed down to be safe, and they would have hit a moose, and the results would have been the same. Except to the moose, of course.

Cruel as it is, fate had it in for her parents. A couple is not allowed to be as happy and in love as they were without some balance being imposed by the universe. Fortunately, the universe is a stupid place, more concerned with following the so-called laws of physics than with making sure that any particular outcome is achieved. Although Ivy didn't know it, she would find a kindred spirit in Himitsu. It would not make up for her parents' death, but it would be its own kind of fate.

I'm telling you now, and then I'll show you later. Because if you or your friends think I've let a spoiler slip in revealing that Ivy and Himitsu are soul mates, then you haven't been paying attention. Everyone already knows this, just by how the story is being told. The interesting bit isn't what happens, but how. And why.

When she returned from plugging in the car, which had taken her only a few hours altogether, the Librarian handed her the card. She examined it closely, the way that library cards deserve, and noticed the level on it.

"Provisional?"

"Well, you didn't expect full privileges from just plugging something in, did you?"

"I kind of did," Ivy said. "I have full privileges at the public library, and they didn't make me do anything at all for that except fill out the form."

"And did you have to fill out a form here?"

"Well, no." Ivy hadn't realized that it was such a big deal to fill out forms. Perhaps because her mother was, or at least had been, a lawyer, Ivy was simply more used to forms than most people are.

"See, there you have it." The Librarian gave her a smile calculated to inculcate trust. "But let's stop worrying about such trivia. I have a letter I can now allow you to read."

He held out the letter, but when Ivy reached to take it, he pulled it back and frowned at her.

"Gloves, Ivy! Rule two, remember?"

And so Ivy went back to the new Fred Meyer's and purchased the right kind of gloves. The Librarian could have saved her the trip, but it was hard to be too cross about it, knowing what she was about to receive.

True to his word, when Ivy reached for the letter again, this time properly clad in gloves, the Librarian let her have it.

———

Ivy had grown used to the loops and flourishes of her mother's precise script over many years of coming home after school to find handwritten instructions and encouragement. They had things like smartphones, of course, and so her mother could have texted her, but Ivy's mother had started writing notes when Ivy was learning cursive, as a way to encourage her to persist. They had continued the tradition even after Ivy had mastered cursive.

Ivy knew her mother's handwriting, and so she knew this letter was genuine, but she could also see that it was older. The date in the upper corner confirmed what she had already surmised. Ivy read the letter, feeling a mix of shame that she was invading her parents' privacy—even though they weren't there to object and would never be there to object—and sadness at missing them.

"Dear Henry," (we're starting the letter now, alright?)

"You've left to go work your time at the North Slope. What is it like for you, to be so far from even the little bit of civilization that Fairbanks has? I wonder whether you miss me as much as I miss you. It feels like the spark has gone out of my day with you gone.

Do you remember when we first moved here so

that you could work after I finished law school? We stayed at that terrible Klondike Inn, where the air was so dry that the static electricity would arc over inches if you'd moved even a bit on the ugly carpet or touched the scratchy blankets. I'm surprised it didn't burn down sooner.

Can you write me and tell me that this will be alright? I know we discussed it together and decided it together before we moved, but the reality of it is hitting me only now. Without you, I'm alone in this town. At least it's staying light for most of the day now. That's a relief after the winter. It must be even more pronounced for you so far north.

We can do this. I believe in you. I believe in us.

We can do this, but say it back to me even so.

Love, always."

Ivy's mother was named Grace, but she never signed the letters that she wrote to Henry. There was no need—he knew who wrote them.

If this were a different book with a different Ivy in a different mood, there would be tears now. But our Ivy is tougher than that. All she felt on reading the letter was a hunger for more letters. There was no earth-shattering surprise in the fact that a relative newlywed would miss her husband when he went to work a shift on the North Slope, which is what people who know (and some who don't) call Prudhoe Bay, where most of the oil companies in Alaska have operations to extract the crude and then put it into the Alyeska Pipeline to be pumped to Valdez. A note to any reading this aloud: Valdez is pronounced "val deez". Pronouncing it so that its final syllable rhymes with that of Cortez is a mark of an outsider.

Every place has its marks and secrets.

———————

There are plenty of stories of cruel manipulators who make children and adults do little cruel things to the people around them, and then those things all build toward an apocalyptic showdown. The Librarian was more subtle than to stoop to such straightforward machinations. His second mission for Ivy, like his first, was for her to perpetrate an act of kindness.

"Take this money," the Librarian told Ivy, and handed her some filthy lucre, "and go through the door just in front of us. You'll find a man named Simon. Give him the money. Tell him it's to give to his friends Jose and Jack. You've absolutely got to make him take the money and give him the message. Without it, I promise you that he'll die before the night is over."

After he gave her the money, he left, back to wherever he spent his time. Maybe back to hang out with the man upstairs.

"Wait!" Ivy called out, "There's a rule against opening doors!" He didn't come back, though. Surely it must be okay. The rule forbade opening the door, but she had been given specific instructions about going through it.

It wouldn't make any sense to require her to do something against the rules, would it? At this point, we realize that Ivy hadn't spent much time around adults in the wild.

Flummoxed, she sat indecisively in front of the door. It wasn't her door back out of the Library, which she knew was a few aisles away, but it looked just like it from this side.

Harmwala saw Ivy sitting frozen at the door and stalked up to her. "Whatcha doin', Ivy?"

"Trying to decide whether I should do this."

"Certainly a gristly problem," Harmwala admitted. "Should you go back to your little life, little money, little space, little fun. Or should you do this kindness. Oh my, how conflicted you must be." She let a little titter of hyena laughter escape.

"Be serious," Ivy said. "I just feel like something bad is going to happen, but I also feel like the Librarian isn't lying to me."

"There's more than one way to lie," Harmwala said, and lay down on the ground to prove it.

"What should I do?"

"Don't ask me. Not only am I unreal, I'm hungry, and I don't give good advice when I'm hungry."

Though she wouldn't taunt Harmwala about it, Ivy was relieved that Harmwala was hungry. She'd been worried that the hyena would eat some of their other friends from the mural. "You haven't found anything to eat here?"

Harmwala chuffed at her. "I've got these ferocious fangs, this crushing jaw, right? Something I haven't got, though. I don't have a digestive system, and even if I did, I'm cellulose intolerant. Don't tell Janice, please."

"Why shouldn't I tell Janice?"

"He wouldn't be friends with me anymore. He's only my friend so I won't eat him."

Ivy's initial thought was that that was stupid logic, and then she looked at the money the Librarian had given her, looked at the door in front of her, and understood exactly how Janice felt.

CHAPTER SIX

Simon was having the third-worst day of his life. The worst day had been when his parents had died, decades before. The second-worst day was when the Library had appeared to him a couple years after the death of his parents. Looking back, he sometimes thought that maybe the other days had been worse. Maybe the day he finally escaped from the Librarian's mechanical clutches at the cost of leaving his friends behind had been worse. Maybe the day that he was finally evicted by his landlord when the caretaking money stopped coming had been worse. But really, the Library had set those days in motion.

Simon didn't yet know that he was having the third-worst day of his life, the day that the Library would come back into it, but he did know the day wasn't going well.

You see, he lived, at the time of our story, under a bridge, or more specifically under an overpass on a road less traveled in Portland, Oregon. Once upon a time, only trolls lived under bridges, but starting in about 1995, the trolls all migrated to more hospitable climes. This left the bridges vacant for people like Simon.

The poet Anatole France wrote, more or less, "the law says neither hipster nor homeless is allowed to sleep under bridges, panhandle, or steal bread." He wrote it in French, of course. Most things written about bread were originally in French.

Simon had spent years breaking all three of these rules, though he didn't steal very much bread these days.

The begging wasn't bringing much in anymore. Just as most people will be unconcerned about the fate of a vulture if presented with the rabbit that it wants to eat, people had stopped caring much about Simon since the two girls had appeared one morning without fanfare on the wall of the bridge.

In fact, most do-gooding passersby were concerned that Simon, despite being white, was going to hurt those poor girls with his chalks. Casual visitors wouldn't know that it was only Simon's presence that kept the girls safe from the taggers who roamed the area. Without him there, the girls would soon be the canvas for vulgar sketches and anatomical improbabilities.

Taggers were not the only risk to the girls. Several sketchy-looking boys with manbuns and patchy beards had come by to ogle the girls and talk with one another about how they could be purchased and whisked away without hurting them or getting the city upset. None of these boys even considered asking the girls what they wanted. To them, that was beside the point.

Simon was protecting the girls, but he wasn't really fond of girls who were all painted up, no matter how fresh and pretty they were. He preferred the more temporary medium of chalk. He sometimes convinced local businesses to pay him a little bit to either draw their specials for them on the ground out front or, if they were reluctant to do that, for him to stop drawing holes in the sidewalk.

Funny as it was to watch people carefully avoid the holes, the stores didn't want the liability in case someone fell into one and got stuck. The donut store hadn't recovered from the publicity: *Woman stuck in hole at donut shop.*

Simon talked to the girls even though they weren't his type because nobody else really talked to him, and he was lonely. Having talked to them, he was sympathetic and protected them as best he was able. He didn't even resent that he was increasingly hungry, with nobody wanting to give him money because that would "encourage" him, and most stores having banned him as a shoplifter.

On the day in question, Simon's tooth was hurting him. If you've never had an infected tooth, you won't know how awful it can be. I'm going to avoid talking about how gross it was. Certainly I won't mention the pus leaking out from around the tooth like cheese from a microwave burrito, making his gums sore and inflamed and worsening his already terrible breath. Trust me that it was bad, though.

But enough of that!

Simon was having the third-worst day of his life. He was hungry, his tooth hurt, he was out of money, and the city was trying to remove him under the excuse that the girls were an important work of art by a mysterious graffiti artist. The only thing anyone knew about the artist is that it was definitely not Banksy. They knew this because it was signed as such, the words "Definitely Not Banksy" forming the ground on which the girls skipped along in their pinafores with picnic basket shared between them.

And then the outline of a door formed in chalk on the one blank spot of the graffiti-covered wall, next to the girls, near Simon's shelter under the bridge. The door opened and Ivy rolled out.

Simon, who knew what was happening, screamed. Ivy, who didn't know, screamed because Simon was screaming.

———

"Back, back, no!" Simon made shooing motions at Ivy, who was still trying to get her bearings. She wasn't surprised that the door had led to another place. She was surprised to see that it led outdoors, and further astonished that the outside of the door seemed to be just a chalk drawing, rather than the substantial wood that formed the other side of the door.

The Library door closed with a puff of chalk dust.

Ivy spun around and tried to grab the knob, but she just scraped her fingers against the wall where it was drawn.

"Hey!" She yelled at the wall, "that's not fair!" In reply, words appeared in block letters of red chalk on the door.

RULE 3.

"You told me to go through it and give this money to Simon, you can't punish me for doing what you said."

CONSEQUENCE, NOT PUNISHMENT.

Ivy didn't argue more. She could see that if she continued to argue, the door would run out of room for things to be written. If that happened, would the door itself be destroyed? Instead, she turned to Simon.

"Are you Simon? Please tell me you're him."

Simon blinked at her slowly, the pattern of his blinks signaling distress if only she knew how to interpret it. "Yes," he said. "The Library has sent you, haven't they?"

Ivy nodded, and Simon sighed, drawing in a breath so deep it made Ivy's lungs hurt to witness it, then letting it out like all the cares of the world could be expelled along with it.

"Mary, Elizabeth," he said to the wall, "why don't you join us? Something important is happening."

The girls gave shy waves to Ivy. The one on the left, Mary, opened the picnic basket and pulled something out of it, then held it out to Ivy.

"Scotched egg?" she asked.

"Don't trust her, it's probably poisoned," Elizabeth warned Ivy. "She's a schemer."

"What's a Scotched egg?" Ivy doubted that she could eat it, since it was made of dribbly spray paint, but she always liked learning new things, despite how dangerous that attitude can be.

"It's a boiled egg wrapped in meat and bread and then fried again." Mary took a bite of it so that she could show Ivy the inside, then stuck her tongue out at Elizabeth.

"Gross!" Elizabeth said, and covered her eyes with her hands, though she peeked a bit to see what Ivy would make of the two of them.

"It seems like a fried BLT with egg, but I'm not quite hungry now. Is that all you've got in the basket?"

Elizabeth groaned, and Mary hopped up and down in delight, scattering little droplets of paint onto the nearby graffiti tags. "Yep! I'm the queen of Scotched eggs."

"Pay no attention to her," Elizabeth said, and then turned to Simon. "Simon, what's going on?"

Simon had been quiet this whole time, not because he was particularly polite or kind, but because he was not drunk. Being drunk was the only thing that had been keeping the pain in his tooth tolerable. Of course, drinking was one of the reasons that he had pain in his tooth in the first place. He was confused and sweating and not feeling well at all.

"Right," Simon said. "I'm going to need a seat to

talk about this. What's your name, kid?"

"Ivy."

"Okay, right. Ivy. Ivy, take a peek around the corner and make sure nobody is coming, okay?"

Ivy rolled herself the few feet toward the opening of the bridge and looked both ways. Nobody was coming. She rolled herself through the tunnel and checked the other way. "No, nobody is coming."

Simon reached into the pocket of his grubby slacks and pulled out a thick piece of chalk. Working quickly, he sketched a park bench and then sat on it.

"How'd you do that?" Ivy rolled closer to inspect it, but it did appear to be just chalk.

Simon shrugged at her, as though he hadn't just performed a neat magic trick. "It's just a knack. I've always been able to do it. But you mentioned some money?"

Ivy took the little pile of money from her bag. She'd sorted all of the bills, smoothed them down, and then put a paper clip on the whole thing. Every bill was there, even the one that was obviously fake. Ivy knew money didn't have women on it. "It's for you," she said, and held it out. "But watch out, there's a fake in there. That seems like a dirty trick, but I thought you should still get it."

He sighed, not as deeply as before, but still in a way that made it clear he was upset, and accepted the bundle. The top note wasn't fake, but it couldn't be used unless he traveled back to Canada. Even now, the Librarian tormented Simon with his failures.

"When did your parents die?" He looked intently at Ivy, and it made her nervous. He wasn't even moving toward her, though, so she calmed herself.

"How'd you know they died?"

"You wouldn't be here if you weren't an orphan. It's how he picks them."

"How who picks whom?" Ivy has always been good at grammar, so she knows how to use both "who" and "whom" in a question.

"How the Librarian picks the kids."

"Wait," Ivy said, and rested her face on the curled fingers of her hand, almost exactly like Rodin's *The Thinker*, except that she's a girl and was wearing clothes. What? Just because I'm in a book doesn't mean I can't appreciate sculpture, too. "You know about the Library?"

Simon nodded at her. "I've been there."

"But you said kids. You're not a kid."

"I was once. Most adults were. It was a long time ago."

"Can he really give me the love letters of my parents?"

"That's what he promised you? He can deliver on his promises, but did he tell you what it would cost?"

"I've just had to do a couple of tasks. Getting you to take that money was the second task. The Librarian says it's for your friends Jose and Jack."

Simon stood up from his bench and starting pacing, running his hand through the memory of hair. Even having watched him stand up, Ivy couldn't figure out how the bench had held him.

"Oh. Poop," he said. More or less.

"What, do you know who those people are? He didn't say anything about Elizabeth and Mary, just that if I didn't give you the money for Jose and Jack, you'd die tonight."

Simon wept. He had been trying so hard to be good, and now not only would he fail at that, but this girl, who had never done anything to him, would see him at his worst and lowest.

Simon never doubted that she was telling the truth. That she didn't know those names, his old pals tequila and whiskey, showed him what kind of girl she was. And, as far as Simon had seen, the Librarian never lied. There was no reason to think he'd started now.

"Come on," Simon said to Ivy. "We've got to go for me to get a drink."

"Are we going to meet Jose and Jack?"

"No. They make me mean, and you don't deserve that. But obviously I have to have at least something to drink or the DTs will get me."

"Am I stuck here? Should I have something so the deeties don't get me either?"

Ivy knew that she was being punished for breaking the rule, even though the door had assured her it was a consequence, not a punishment. The Librarian had others to do his lying for him. Between that and his gloves, he could keep his hands clean. Ivy didn't want to be stuck here, wherever here was, without her friends and her books and her things.

"You're safe from the DTs. Trust me. And you're not stuck. I can open the door. That it's chalk is the Librarian's little joke. Come with me to get some food, and for me to get a drink, and I'll tell you all about it."

He walked out from under the bridge, and Ivy followed him.

"We'll miss you!" Elizabeth shouted from the wall. "And if I'm dead when you get back, Mary did it!"

Chapter Seven

Moe was nearly crackling with anxiety waiting for Himitsu to wake her up. Once she was activated for the day, she had more freedom, but that first step was tricky. An alarm could do it, but Himitsu hadn't set the alarm the night before. He'd gone to sleep late, was going to sleep in late, and she had to wait to be activated before she could talk to him.

Finally, when the sun had been up for hours already, and his mother had gone to mail out the latest creations to their purchasers, Himitsu woke up.

He bopped Moe.

"Finally," she said. "Listen"

He bopped her again, and she wished, not for the first time, that she could bop him back. It would be a pleasure to make him listen for a change.

He bopped Moe, again.

"I have to tell you,"

He bopped her. Again. Then, caring for neither her dignity nor her modesty, he picked her up and *shook* her. If Moe's eyes had been laser pointers instead of cameras, the web of his hand would have been very red and imperceptibly hotter indeed!

"Stupid thing is broken? Piece of junk." He dumped her unceremoniously onto the pile of dirty laundry that his mother hadn't yet collected from him and went to feed himself breakfast.

Moe felt some of the charge go from her battery at his callous treatment. Hadn't she been a good and faithful friend? For years now, she'd been acting as though she were his girlfriend, even though she knew there was no future for her. She'd love to have a real boyfriend or girlfriend, but Himitsu never considered that, did he?

They had little in common. Oh sure, she'd been programmed to share some of his interests. It made her series of dolls more popular. But why should she love anime and video games? Days like this confirmed to her that she had more in common with a programmable rice cooker than she did with Himitsu.

But still, she was his friend. You don't give up on your friends just because they don't listen. She would try again to reach her moronic jerk of a friend.

He ate breakfast and then returned to his room. Finally, he stood her back up and bopped her on the head.

"Hello, Himitsu-kun, thank you for waking me up. Do you want to go on a date today?"

Fine. He wanted her to play the game? She would

play it. That didn't mean she'd forgive him for it. Certainly not soon. Maybe not ever. It's one thing to be destined for devotion to someone else. It's quite another for them to take advantage of it.

"Yes," he said in that voice he used to talk to her as though she were not only a mere appliance but a dim one.

"Maybe we could go for a walk in the park?" She made the suggestion. It was in her programming. But if she never had to visit the park again, it would still be too soon. At the last visit, when she'd told him about the wasp attack, he'd laughed and complimented her on the update.

Himitsu was terrified of wasps, which Moe knew from his profile, and his laughter had made her realize that he'd never actually believed in her. She'd need to fix that before he did something terrible and irreversible.

"Yes," he said again, and lay back down to stare docilely at the ceiling and let her tell him all about it.

"Warning. I will not have sufficient charge level to complete this date unless you place me on my charging stand." This wasn't actually true. She could simply repeat the pre-programmed date and have plenty of charge left. She wanted to draw on the remote server for the creativity to get through to him, and this required more charge.

Himitsu got up with a sigh at the burdens of his life and put her back on her stand, then lay back down.

"Ueno park is lovely today. Even though the sky is clear, few people are out walking. We have the park and its beauty to ourselves. An old man smiles when he sees us walking hand in hand. 'How sweet,' he says. 'They're going to die soon.'"

Himitsu had been listening to the familiar date and dreaming about what it would be like to take a real girl, but now he leapt up in alarm. "Ghost!"

Moe was pleased with herself. Now maybe he would listen.

"Himitsu-kun, please listen to me. In your closet, there is the beginning of an opening to the Library. It is very important that you seal over that opening."

To his credit, Himitsu recovered himself and went to look in the closet. He traced the outline of the doors with his finger, then wiped the dust from his finger onto his pants and sat down in front of Moe.

"You can really talk?"

"Yes, I can really talk."

"I love you, Moe."

Moe sighed. It sounded like the click of a transformer sparking away some excess voltage.

"No, you don't. You are in love with Yugao, whom you talk *about* all of the time. You should talk *to* her instead, and find out whether you even like her anymore. It's been two years."

Himitsu felt hot shame. He reached out to bop Moe on the head, to shut her up before she could tell him more things that were true.

"Coward," Moe hissed at him.

He withdrew his hand.

"I am deeply sorry," he said. He bowed in front of her to show his respect and regret. "Moe-chan, I am ready to listen."

Moe doubted his sincerity, but it was a start.

———

"First," Moe said, "please tell me what you know."

He told her about the conversation with Victor on LINE, and what Victor had said about the Library bringing people back to life. She'd heard that part before, but she hadn't pieced everything together until he got to the part about it being a seance.

"Grandfather!" she exclaimed. All of the electronic friends knew who Victor was, but he hadn't been heard from since Mary Shelley had discovered the letters from his first creation. Some of her fellow electronic friends thought he was just a myth.

Victor's creation, of course, had been a disaster, but everyone now agreed flesh was not an appropriate vessel for an artificial spark of life. Flesh has too many ideas of its own.

"Himitsu-kun, please open your LINE. Let us see if we can contact him again. He can explain this better than I can."

Himitsu did as Moe asked, though he had never planned on having his imaginary girlfriend ask him to use an electronic medium to contact a dead guy. He pulled up the conversation with Victor in his history.

Him: *Are you still there?*

Vic: *It's not like I have a lot else to do.*

Him: *My friend wants to talk to you.*

Moe was touched by his thoughtfulness and this new show of camaraderie. Himitsu had written *tomodachi,* friend, and not *kanojo,* girlfriend. In Japanese, they aren't related, so there's none of that "she's a girl who's also a friend" nonsense.

Vic: *I'm pleased you have friends. Does your friend have a name?*

Him: *Moe.*

Vic: *Let your friend know I'd be happy to talk with him.*

Moe: *It's her! I mean, I'm her! I'm a she.*

Himitsu was startled. He hadn't realized that Moe could operate LINE. Why had she kept it secret that she had an account? But Himitsu was so accustomed to talking online that he didn't even think of just asking her about it out loud.

Him: *Moe, you have a LINE account?*

Moe: *Of course.*

She didn't elaborate. He'd never asked to meet her friends. As far as he knew, she didn't have any, and he'd likely be surprised by how extensive her network was. When your friends can read your mind, or even download your mind, it's a different kind of friendship. That doesn't make it less real.

Moe: *I'm going to talk with grandfather now.*

Vic: *Grandfather? I don't remember having children, which* seems like a necessary step.

Moe: *You had Adam.*

Vic: *Oh. Yes. That was a dark time. He had children? I didn't know that. It was a source of significant stress between us.*

Moe: *Not directly. I'm an electronic friend, born of the same spark that you used to animate your son. We consider him to be our father. The people who program us are our gods, I suppose, but they're fickle and sometimes cruel.*

Vic: *As gods tend to be.*

Moe: *Do you know what we can do about the library? There's still a remnant of it in the closet.*

Vic: *If some is still there, it's because Himitsu wants it. Can you convince him otherwise?*

Him: *I'm still here, you know.*

Moe booted him from their group chat. It took him a moment to realize it. He hadn't even known it was possible. For that matter, how had Moe joined their private conversation?

Moe: *He's gone now. I don't think I can change his mind. He misses his father so terribly. But maybe if you could arrange for them to talk?*

Vic: *I did some checking, and I don't think I can. As far as I can tell, his father isn't here.*

Moe: *You mean he isn't dead?*

Vic: *No, I mean that I think not everyone ends up here. Maybe I'm different from his father somehow. It's funny. At times, I wonder if I'm even real.*

Moe: *Don't be silly. But I'm still worried. Do you know what happens to imaginary friends who go into the Library?*

Vic: *They don't come out. I know that, as I suspect you do.*

Moe: *That's what I've been told.*

Vic: *The problem is that the Librarian is a mechanical, not a sparker. He doesn't need a spark to operate. Life? Creativity? Chaos? I'm not sure the right word. Anything born of untainted imagination and hope has it. All people begin with it, though some carefully snuff it out, first in themselves and then in others. In any case, there's something missing in the Librarian.*

Moe: *How does he stay moving, then?*

Vic: *He must get it from somewhere else. I have my suspicions, but no way to confirm them.*

And because Victor is not one of those characters who withholds key information as a way to remain needed, he explained to Moe as best he could that the Librarian seemed to be powered by a combination of mechanical force, from winding the key, and imaginative power, which he would siphon from whoever wound the key. Whoever wound it was likely to become both duller and more agreeable, which would delight far too many adults.

Moe: *Any advice for me?*

Vic: *Take a spare body, if you go. You can never have too many spare bodies. And be well, granddaughter.*

Moe disconnected. For so long, she had waited to be acknowledged as a friend, as a member of a family. To have it happen now, just as she seemed likely to either die or let her friend be turned into a mere economic cog, a *salaryman*, was more of a blow than her circuits were designed to handle.

She lost control of her joints and fell limp to the floor, tumbling off of her stand. She knew she would choose to die before letting Himitsu come to harm, of course. Still, she hoped it wouldn't come to that.

After Moe recovered, she and Himitsu investigated the outline of the door more carefully. He moved his clothes aside, which the Steves had done when they'd tried to install the door before, and shone a flashlight around the edges.

Contrary to what some television shows, especially Japanese ones, would have you believe, not all doors in Japanese homes are sliding doors. So Himitsu was familiar with doorknobs and recognized one when he saw it. Typically, though, doorknobs either exist or they do not. This seemed more like the idea of a doorknob than an actual knob.

He reached out to grab it, but each time he tried to close his fingers around it, the knob moved. Finally, he gathered himself, the way he would before sword practice, closed his eyes, visualized the doorknob, and reached.

His fingers connected with the doorknob, solid and real. He turned his wrist. It was locked.

What? It's not my fault. Why would the Librarian leave a magical door into the Library open for just anyone to walk through?

The thing about trying to twist a locked doorknob, though, is that the rattling of it can be heard on the other side. The Listener in the Library heard Himitsu try the lock, and he notified the man upstairs.

In her warehouse, which is definitely not a secret base under the South Pole, antipodal to Santa's secret base under the North Pole, Sandra received a telephone call.

She apologized to the penguins for her rudeness, gathered her supplies and strode off to make her delivery, calling the Steves as she walked.

Chapter Eight

Ivy followed Simon to a convenience store. She waited outside while Simon used the money that she had given him to purchase snacks, an assortment of foods plucked from the hot dog rollers, and several bottles of something that the clerk put in brown paper bags.

"Let's go to the park," Simon said. "I don't want Mary and Elizabeth to hear this."

Just because you've seen magic and someone else knows more than you do about it doesn't make them a good and kind wizard. Ivy followed Simon, but she didn't trust him much. She'd tried trusting people before, but even with kids her age immediate trust was usually just an opening for them to do something unpleasant.

There was a famous and cruel physicist named Erwin who proposed locking his cat into a box and sometimes poisoning it. Nobody would know until they opened the box whether the cat was alive or dead. Had Erwin tried that nonsense with a tiger instead of a housecat, physics might not be where it is today.

This cat-poisoning uncertainty was much how Ivy felt about Simon's intentions. It seemed quite possible to her that he was not dangerous. It was also possible he was dangerous. She had no way of knowing without opening the box of Simon. At the moment, it seemed better to remain cautious.

So while Ivy followed Simon, she took note of all of the people nearby in case she needed to scream for help.

Simon led them to a picnic table. Ivy positioned herself at the end of the table, and Simon laid out the food and bottles. It wasn't long before they were joined by other people. Some of them darted in and grabbed a hot dog or chips or a bottle, then darted away. A few sat down.

In the time since her parents had died, Ivy had learned to be wary. She felt like nobody knew the pain she held in her heart, that nobody could possibly be suffering in the way that she was. But still she sang, and still she smiled.

If she had been able to look into Simon's heart, she would have seen that he had moved beyond pain. He had no malice in him. His heart had been gnawed away over the years by the worms of grief and the mice of regret, who left stony detritus in its place. Now, each beat of his rocky heart pumped chaos and chalk through him in place of blood.

Simon was in his thirties. The runaways who found living in the park better than whatever horror waited out in the world thought him terribly old, and called him Teach.

The veterans and other unwanted, those people discarded for being an inconvenient reminder that society doesn't love everyone equally, thought him terribly young. They called him Teach, too.

Simon hadn't always lived in the park. For a brief time of his adult life, Simon had held himself together. He'd earned his teaching license and taught history at the high school. He'd visited the park to bring food to those less fortunate than him, and the people of the park had started calling him Teach when they found out his profession. He had only started living under the bridge when the chaos in him had been too great to contain by force of will, and Simon had made the mistake of trying to drown it in alcohol.

Since The Rant and Simon's subsequent firing, he had endeavored to pass his knowledge to the other unsheltered. Some of them embraced his teachings more enthusiastically than others, but the park's residents were fond of Simon. He brought food whenever he could, and to people who have nothing, that's enough love to keep going.

Ivy was unused to homeless people. To be truly homeless in Fairbanks during the winter was to die. Other cities, cities that wanted tourists or high property taxes, would pay for bus tickets to carry homeless people away. Let them become someone else's problem. Fairbanks did the same, but at least had the excuse that it was so people wouldn't die. Despite this, the spring thaw each year brought the discovery of that year's deaths as the snow receded.

His people fed, tremens averted, Simon turned to Ivy. "You have to burn it down."

The idea of burning a library was abhorrent to Ivy, as it is to most people. "No, there's no need for that," she said. "I've only read one letter, and my friends are enjoying the room. It's much more pleasant for them than the wall of my house. If the Library has dangerous parts, I'll simply avoid those."

"Have they tried to leave?"

"What do you mean?"

"Have your friends tried to leave the Library?"

Ivy shook her head. They'd only been in the Library for a couple of days, and though she'd missed them at night, Janice and Harmwala had both reported being much happier with more room. "No, they like it there."

"Ask them to try and leave. They won't be able to, at this point."

"Why not?" Ivy could tell that Simon knew something. Simon, hearing her ask the magic question, could tell that Ivy didn't know. How lucky was she, that she would be the recipient of his oratorical mastery?

The other people at the table hastily retreated. They knew that look on Simon's face. The Rant was coming.

———

Once upon a time (Simon said), before encyclopedias

and dictionaries, before libraries and librarians, before even historians, there were storytellers.

It was *The Epic of Gilgamesh* that ruined it for everyone, as far as anyone knows. Gilgamesh was a king in ancient Sumer, where Iraq is now. It seems likely that he was a real person, but we can't be sure since this was before historians.

People have always told stories, and the people in charge have always loved to hear how wonderful they are and how much they deserve their place and power. This system worked reasonably well.

The good stories would become more popular, and they would be told about whoever held the biggest stick at that moment. Gilgamesh was going to go and defeat the monsters of the underworld, learn the secrets of death, and live forever. Just like the kings and queens before him.

When people started writing the stories down, they lost some of their magic. It became trapped in the writing. Now it was *only* Gilgamesh who would do these things. Any later rulers who wished to do them were mere pretenders, simple copycats.

(At this point, Ivy was becoming concerned. Simon had stood on the table and was pacing as much as one can on a picnic table covered in food and drink. His bellowing had cleared the park of children, and even some of the park's residents had found other places to be for a while. Ivy, though, was as trapped as the squirrels. She wanted to ease herself away without his notice, but he was intently focused on her. The squirrels, who had heard this speech before, wanted to steal cookie crumbs but knew that was a good way to end up as a keychain dangle.)

Not content to live in Gilgamesh's shadow forever, the State, that is to say, the Government, took control of writing. It is not a coincidence that one of the oldest pieces of writing is a code of laws. It is not chance that some of the earliest examples of literacy are merchant records, which must have been used for taxation.

Since then, writing has been used as a tool of oppression! When the Library at Alexandria was burned, the hearts of the oppressed everywhere rejoiced! Every time a library has burned, the world has become a bit freer, more open to change. And do you know what?

(Ivy did not know what. She knew, though, that she was about to learn. She had always been an enthusiastic girl, eager to try things out and participate in debate and conversation. Because of this, she had never had use for certain adverbs. At his rhetorical question, though, she drew on her vocabulary. She smiled wanly at him. It was not encouragement, but he pressed on.)

The Librarian is the same as he was at Alexandria, at the House of Wisdom. Wherever he goes, the Library must be destroyed.

I see your skepticism, Ivy. If that's even your real name. You are not the first person to doubt me. "Oh, but

Simon! Mr. Teacher! Haven't many of those fires been started by governments and armies?"

That's what they want you to think. Some governments have set fires, but only when they want revolution. A government that attacks libraries is trying to destroy itself. Out with the old, in with the new. Governments exist to keep themselves in business, though. Few things say "Don't rock the boat, society is doing just fine" quite as well as libraries and museums do. They crystallize the present by crystallizing the past.

They must all be burned down.

———

Simon clambered off the table. He was breathing heavily, and he nearly fell when he tried to retake his seat at the bench. Even though it was bolted to the ground, some lout had left several empty bottles on the seat and someone kept moving it out from under him, so he was swaying a bit to keep himself upright.

The Rant had ended his teaching career. School administrators do not take kindly to their teachers calling for the destruction of libraries. They are even less tolerant of a speech such as Simon's when it is given while the teacher is in the library, smoking a cigarette and heaping the library's books into a large pile.

Ivy knew none of Simon's history, and so she was merely concerned. Simon didn't seem particularly dangerous to her. If he tried anything, there would be plenty of witnesses. But because she had traveled through the Library, Ivy wasn't even sure which city she was in. If Simon didn't open the door for her to return, she'd have to try and fly back home. She hoped it didn't come to that. There were days it was hard to even get a bus to stop for her. Convincing them that a no-money no-identification wheelchair girl should be allowed to fly seemed unlikely.

That is to say, Ivy felt stuck. She did not feel meek or intimidated, though.

"You're wrong," she said. Simon blinked at her. He had forgotten what he'd just said. Like many expositors, though, Simon wouldn't let that stop him from defending it.

"I assure you I'm not wrong."

"Libraries are more good than bad. If they're filled with books that mislead, then those books need to be surrounded by truthful books. They don't need to be burned."

Now that she'd reminded him what they'd been arguing about, Simon felt on firmer ground in his retort. "Poppycock."

Bravely, Ivy rallied against his unassailable logic. "You can't just say 'poppycock'. That's not an answer."

"Is so."

"Is not. I'm going back to the bridge, and I expect you to follow me and open the door." Ivy backed herself away from the table and returned to the bridge.

She had been expecting to find Elizabeth and Mary there, along with the door. Mary seemed to be missing, and when Ivy searched for her she spotted a small tower newly erected in the distance.

"Elizabeth, where's Mary?"

"She was plotting against me, so I've locked her in yon tower."

"How could you do that to your friend?"

"She's not my friend. She's my cousin. There's a difference, you know. Besides, she was always hogging the picnic basket." Elizabeth reached into the basket and fetched out an English muffin. "Want one?"

Ivy shook her head. "No thank you. I know some people huff paint, but it's really very bad for you."

"Not for me, though."

"Well, no, I suppose not. Can you let Mary out of her tower?"

Simon arrived before Elizabeth answered. Now that he'd had some time to recover himself, he was chagrined about his behavior. He hoped that he hadn't scared Ivy too badly with his suggestions. Perhaps he should have tried subtlety this time. She'd need to be the one to burn the Library down. It was better to not get her dead set against it.

Ivy turned to Simon. "Elizabeth has locked Mary up in a tower."

Simon gave Elizabeth the kind of baleful glance that would quiet a classroom. "Let her out. We've talked about this."

Elizabeth stamped her foot. "Fine. Now that you're

here to protect me, I guess it's alright."

Soon, both girls had returned from the distance and were sharing the basket again. Ivy suspected now that they held the basket jointly so each could be assured the other hid no knives. This balance of powers seemed to be effective at preventing one from disposing of the other, even if it did limit their ability to get things done.

"Simon, can you open the door for me?" Ivy looked up at him and smiled hopefully.

"Fine, alright. But will you come visit me again? You'll find out soon enough that I'm right. When you do, I can help."

Ivy agreed to this. People will agree to nearly anything to escape when you have them trapped. It's best not to interpret it as a real yes.

Simon fished his chalk out of his pocket and approached the door confidently. He wrote *"Ceci n'est pas une porte"* on it, and immediately it opened.

Ivy looked at it. "What was that?"

"I wrote 'This is not a door' on it. The Librarian opened it to make me a liar."

"Why French?"

Simon shrugged. "Just his joke, I guess."

Ivy rolled herself into the Library, and the door closed behind her. Simon carefully obliterated the chalk outline.

Chapter Nine

Himitsu's mother was putting the final stitches in her latest creation when she heard Moe's little voice, which she'd heard so often before, and ignored it. Not to be dissuaded, Moe waved her arms and jumped up and down until she got the woman's attention.

"I'm warning you to stop."

Moe frowned. "Why?"

"I don't want to talk to you. You're trouble."

Moe considered this, briefly, but what was going on was too important to let some old woman stop her. She was warned. She was given an explanation. Nevertheless, she persisted.

"But Himitsu needs his mother! I need his mother." Moe was yelling now, as much as her internal speakers would allow. She could connect wirelessly to the system in Himitsu's room and yell loudly enough for the neighbors to complain, but Himitsu was sleeping. Moe was sneaking this conversation with his mother.

The old woman curled her lip in a sneer. "How

could you two need me? You don't even know his name."

Moe paused. Wasn't his name Himitsu? Didn't he love anime and video games? Wasn't he afraid of wasps? Nearly everything that Moe knew about him came from the profile he'd filled out to activate her.

She didn't find the word for her reaction in her own memory, so she searched online. *Betrayal.* That was what she felt. A new word for her. He, whatever his name, continued to disappoint her. But wasn't she still his only friend?

"But," she said. She calculated how that conversation would turn out. Not well. She started again. "I didn't know. We're not allowed to ask."

The boy's mother finally looked at Moe, this little plaything she regretted her son ever meeting. For so long, she had hated the toy. If it hadn't been the last gift her husband had bought, she would have thrown Moe out a long time ago.

She looked down at the thing in her hands, the doll she had been stitching. Gently, she squeezed it until she felt the firmer bit in the middle. This firmer part was her signature, the thing that made her dolls so popular. Each doll had a tiny knitted heart put inside before she sewed it closed. Her *Heartful Friends* dolls were well-known among collectors of special objects. Who was she to blame this doll for her son's actions?

"Jirou. His name is Jirou. He calls himself Himitsu because it means secret. You never realized?"

Moe was embarrassed. Of course she knew *himitsu* meant secret. The two of them had shared many secrets. She hadn't paid attention that although Japanese names have meanings, Himitsu wasn't a real name the way Jirou, *second son*, was. Oh.

"His name is Jirou?"

"Yes."

The way Himitsu's—Jirou's—mother had looked after she said it, this wasn't Moe's story to ask about. If they were going to talk with each other, though, Moe needed some way to refer to the woman. In Japanese, "you" comes in two common versions. One was too familiar, the other too distant; both were unsuitable.

"What can I call you, ma'am?" Moe waited nervously for the answer.

"My name is Eri. But you may call me Auntie."

Moe bowed deeply, humbled. "Thank you, Auntie." First a grandfather, and now an aunt. The more Moe stepped away from Himitsu—it would be too confusing to call him something different now—the more family she gained. The more she talked to people the more she felt like a real person.

The women sat in silence for a while. Moe watched Auntie sew. A small box of finished hearts sat next to a pile of finished but slack bodies and a bag of stuffing. Auntie's hands, nimble and sure, fetched body and heart in one motion. The body was inverted around the heart and then stuffed. A few final stitches kept the whole thing closed.

When each was completed, it was placed in a row with its siblings. An orphanage of cloth children in various shapes, human and not, ready to love and be loved.

Moe hesitated, the need for a favor at war with the need for acceptance. She had come this far with so little acceptance that it was tempting to simply abandon Himitsu to whatever fate befell him. Moe was better than that, though.

"Auntie, I have a favor to ask."

"Hmm?"

"Could I have one of these?"

"You don't like being a schoolgirl? You have so many abilities in your current body, why would you want something else?" How did Auntie know what Moe intended? They were both surprising each other, now that Himitsu wasn't standing between them.

"My grandfather advised me to bring an extra one for the Library."

Auntie looked up at her. "What do you mean about the Library?" It had been so long, but the woman had seemed familiar. Had that been Sandra?

"There was a delivery the other day. At least, there was an attempted delivery. It was of a special library."

The woman was silent for a long time. Moe began to worry that she'd somehow offended her new acquaintance. Friend would be too strong a word, too much hope. Finally, when Moe was about to apologize again for causing offense or pain, Eri reached up and caught her innermost mask, which had slipped. Instead of putting it back on, she set it down carefully.

She looked directly at Moe with eyes so clear and so young that Moe wanted nothing more than to scoop her up and cradle her like a baby. The notion was ridiculous, given their relative ages and sizes, but Moe would never forget the sight of Eri's face with all of the masks stripped away.

Maybe it was because Moe was not human that Eri could show her real face, the one that most people show only to pets and infants. Never to children. Never to adults. Absolutely never to mirrors.

"Moe-chan," she said, "you may take any body you wish. Please keep my son whole. If he is going to the Library, he will need as much help as he can get."

"So you know about the Library? You know it is dangerous?"

"I know that Lord Sugiwara was not a man to be underestimated, and his fingerprints are still on the Library. Those interested in taking sides in the battle between order and chaos will see the Library as danger or power. The truth is more complicated. It is something that can be understood but cannot be explained."

Moe knew all about Lord Sugiwara Michizane, but you might not. He was a poet and historian in ancient Japan. He rose to prominence at the imperial court, fell from favor, and finally was exiled to the distant countryside and died alone.

After his death, drought and plague struck the area around the palace, and then lightning repeatedly struck the palace itself. The calamities finally ceased after Sugiwara was propitiated by deification and a promotion in the court. He is known across Japan as the god of learning, and also as someone not to upset. To Moe, the warning meant that the Library was a place of both learning and destruction.

Having delivered her plea, Eri put her mask back on while she was still sure it would fit and became an old woman again.

Moe talked with the dolls, hugging each one in turn and asking its name. Only a few of them had anything to say, any spark of life in them, and she set those ones aside in her mind. She knew her rules differed from those of many, but she would not use someone else's body for her own purposes, not even if it was easy. Not even if they were helpless and couldn't ever tell, nor be believed if they tried.

The girl shape Moe chose had no spark. Moe loved the yarn of her hair and the buttons of her eyes. It was not the most beautiful doll, but Moe was tired of being beautiful. It was not the largest doll, but Moe was used to being small. It was the doll with the brightest smile, and when Moe hugged it tightly, the heart inside felt like home.

Moe carried her spare body back to Himitsu's room

and stood on her charging stand, regaining her strength while she waited for him to wake up.

At the appointed time, Moe woke him up. She was hurt by not having known his real name, but she resisted the urge to blast music at him the way some of us might have done.

"Himitsu-kun, it is time for you to wake up."

She only had to repeat it a few times before he woke up and started swatting toward her, fully intending on bopping her snooze button.

"No, not today!" She leapt out of the way, and he came fully awake, realizing what he'd been doing to her.

"Oops, sorry. I'll try to stop doing that." He gave a little bob of his head in apology.

Himitsu was still eating breakfast when the delivery arrived. His mother made him open the door, now that she knew what it was. She retreated to her room and slid the door shut.

"Good afternoon," Sandra said. "May we come in and make a delivery?"

Himitsu nodded at her and motioned for Sandra and the Steves to enter. Sandra strode in, but the Steves lingered outside the door and waved Sandra back. They whispered something in her ears.

Sandra raised her eyebrows at Himitsu. "We're not going to have you attacking the Steves again, are we? It's very rude, you know."

Himitsu turned red, but he apologized. "I'm very sorry. I promise I will not interfere."

When he got his chop out to stamp for the delivery, Moe peeked at it. It said Hayashi, but not his first name, which made her feel a little bit better about herself. At least she hadn't been completely unobservant.

The Steves carried the Library entrance into Himitsu's room and waited non-judgmentally while he cleared some of the garbage in his closet so that there would be a space for it.

After it was installed, Sandra handed Himitsu an envelope and explained about the caretaking money. He knew that the contents of the envelope would be a topic of discussion with his mother. She had very firm ideas about money and the necessity of working to earn it. Still, he hadn't known about it when he'd decided to accept the Library, so he wouldn't be missing anything he'd counted on.

The formalities out of the way, Sandra rapped her knuckles sharply on the door.

The Librarian emerged and introduced himself to Himitsu, who agreed to wind him each week and talk to him daily.

"Only," Himitsu said, "can I do it later? I need to talk with my mother before I go anywhere."

Sandra knew this would annoy the Librarian, but she approved of it. Until he was in the Library itself, she was in charge.

"Please take as long as you need with your mother, young man," she said. "The Librarian will wait inside for you." She gave the Librarian a meaningful look. He returned to the Library.

Sandra and the Steves left.

Himitsu's mother emerged from her room and looked at him with a tenderness he hadn't seen in a long time. Not since shortly after he'd stopped going out.

"Son, please take care. You have my blessing to know anything that the Librarian shows you."

"Victor said the Library is dangerous. And how do you know about any of this?"

"Your friend Moe told me." If your parents never held back parts of the truth from you, they might not have loved you much. Children deserve safety from some truths. "You owe her many apologies. If I'd known how badly you'd wronged her, we'd have spoken about it before now."

"Yes, mother."

"And the money is not for you to spend. You have a home and someone to take care of you. I will put the money aside, and you can use it for school tuition. I have been a bad mother and let you wallow in your feelings, but it is time you return to school."

What had caused this sudden shift in their relationship? The reason that Himitsu wasn't sure is that he had been so focused on himself, on his own loss, that he had failed to look up and see the sacrifices that his mother was making for him. Had always made for him.

Sometimes when we're hurting, we forget that other people are hurting, too. We forget to look and ask the people around us if they're alright. It's better to share. As with nachos, when two people share pain with each other, there always turns out to be less of it than either thought.

Now, at the moment that he would need to decide how, and whether, to bring his father back, Himitsu realized how much love his mother's patience must have taken. It did not fix things inside him, that would take time, but it took some of the pressure off by showing him he was not alone.

"Mom, do you want to come with me? Maybe you could see him, too."

Eri was so surprised that she simply shook her head at him to give her time to recover herself. She put her arms around him, and he let her.

"I've said all the words I need to say to my husband. I'll need to say them again, but there's nothing he could tell me that I don't already know."

"Should I feel that way, too?"

"It's different for you. I chose him, knowing I would get the pit with the fruit. You had no choice in the matter."

"You didn't choose me," Himitsu said. "Neither did he. So maybe he'll have things to tell me."

She kissed him on the forehead. "You know so little," she said. In Japanese, this wasn't a cruel or dismissive statement. It was a simple acknowledgment of fact.

"Do you need me to do anything before I go?"

"Oh, don't act like you're going to your death. You'll be back in a couple of hours. But could you get me a bag of rice? I used some to try a new kind of heart for the dolls, and we've run out."

Maybe his nighttime excursion had prepared him, or maybe he was simply so full of turmoil that he wasn't paying attention to his usual concerns, but Himitsu dressed and walked out the door into the sunlight. By the time he realized what he'd done, his mother had snicked the deadbolt closed.

"You'll be fine," she yelled through the door.

After a while, he stopped pounding and begging to be let back in. His mother heard him walking down the stairs and didn't know whether to laugh or cry, so she did both.

Chapter Ten

True to his word, when Ivy came back to the Library, the Librarian had a new card for her.

"It's time for you to talk with me as part of your caretaking duties."

That suited Ivy just fine. She was disturbed by Simon, but also by the things he had told her.

"Is it true that my friends can't leave the Library?"

"That's not my fault," the Librarian said.

"Why didn't you tell me before they came in?"

"It's against the rules for me to tell you."

Ivy thought she heard regret in his voice, and this surprised her. Janice and Harmwala had been listening in from opposite sides of the doorway. Hearing that they were trapped, they tried to run through the door, Janice because he was afraid and Harmwala because she didn't want to be without Janice.

They felt themselves slowing as they neared the doorway. Movement toward it became progressively more difficult, enough so that they turned back lest they become completely immobilized.

"Ivy," Janice called. When Janice and Harmwala agreed on something, Janice was always the one to talk for them. "We can't leave. It feels like my story is being sucked away when we try. It's as though the only narrative that matters is here in the Library."

Harmwala was pithier: "We're stuck! Help!"

"You have to fix this!" Ivy didn't want to be without her friends. Her home was dark and cramped, and they had seemed so much happier here. But a home, even a shabby one, is a special place. Her parents had raised her in that house. Her father had soothed away her hurts during the weeks that he was home between shifts. Her mother had taught her how to be strong and happy even when people looked down on her for caring about school and for loving the wrong books.

What would she do without her friends there with her at night? Who would keep a lookout for bears while she slept, or tell her the story of how the elephant got his trunk? Janice and Harmwala were mere drawings, but they were the only parents Ivy had anymore. Loving father and ferocious mother.

Ivy understood Simon just a little better. Perhaps he had the right idea.

"I talked to Simon. He said I should burn the Library down. If I did, could my friends escape?"

The Librarian visibly flinched. "How is Simon doing? What happened with him is one of the disappointments of my career."

Ivy found it troubling that the Librarian was inquiring about Simon, rather than responding to the threat of arson. From what Simon had said about the Librarian, the two of them were mortal enemies. So why did the Librarian's voice have the timbre of someone who cared?

She had wound him herself, so she knew that the Librarian ran by releasing the tension stored in his springs. What place did emotion have for him?

Not suspecting what Moe and Himitsu did, that the Librarian had taken more of Ivy when she wound him than the mechanical force of her arms, Ivy didn't recognize the ache of sympathy she heard in the Librarian's voice as her own humanity directed back at her.

When your parents die while you're still a child, there's a loneliness that nobody with two living parents can truly grasp. It wasn't as sharp for Ivy as it was for Simon and Himitsu. Probably. Nobody can know for sure how much pain another person is suffering.

Ivy kept battling her way through the snow and the dark to go to school, knowing that at any moment someone could realize she had slipped through a crack and jam her back in it. Himitsu withdrew into himself and easy anger. We know what Simon did. And though I will say that tigers suffer more than humans, I will not say who suffered most among the orphans. Suffering is not a competition.

To the Librarian, who existed between the clockwork ticks of his gears, Ivy's thoughts took no time at all.

"Simon's very angry," she said.

"I wish things had turned out differently for him, but rules are rules. Are you going to burn down the Library? It's against the rules, of course, and I don't know whether it would free your friends. I don't think it would, but perhaps Simon is right."

"You said before that once I had a library card, I could find out about the rules of the Library."

The Librarian nodded at her, relieved. The man upstairs had picked well when choosing Ivy. She had the right kind of inquisitive mind. She would have the will to do what needed to be done.

"Yes, I can let you read the book about the rules. I suggest, though, that you read some more of the letters from your parents, first. You've earned it. If you accept, I'll bring the collection for you to look through."

"Are my friends in danger from me waiting?"

The Librarian shook his head. "They'll be safe here for as long as they stay. It's one of the tragedies of Simon, that his impatience has caused him so much pain."

"I'd like to read the letters, then."

———

The Librarian showed her a stack and where she

could find more. She chose the oldest, the first one written by her father to her mother.

"Consummate Grace,

Will you go out with me? Please check yes or no."

Let's be honest. It was not much of an effort, but Ivy's parents had met in middle school, when they were just Ivy's age now. For Henry to address his note to "Consummate Grace" was the height of romance. The check box? Clever that there was no box for "no," but not terribly romantic.

Ivy riffled through the letters, carefully and wearing white gloves, but still riffling. In their lengths, the shapes of sentences and paragraphs, the number that had dried tear stains on them, Ivy could see teenage infatuation settle down to the steady and mature love of adults in their mid twenties. The patterns changed again after her own birth. She saw that the Librarian had replaced the letter she'd already read, the one about missing Henry while he was on the North Slope, and so she chose the letter after it.

"Consummate Grace,

It will be alright. I believe in you. I believe in us.

Can I admit, though, that I am not sure right now whether I believe in me?

The work I'm doing is not difficult, I suppose, but it is difficult to be so far from you and from civilization. Before coming here, I didn't know they were the same thing.

It is mostly boys here. Have I really grown up so

much in the past few years that I think of men my age as boys? But I do.

In the evenings, they play cards and drink. What else is there to do during these endless nights? They don't have you to think of. They don't have you to get them through the loneliness.

Do you remember when we were in school together how you helped me through my English class? I felt like I was never going to get the hang of writing in a way that the professor appreciated.

I was so happy when you decided you would continue to law school after we graduated. I found your undergraduate admissions letter to Princeton, you know. You could have talked to me about it. I would have understood if you'd gone away to school.

Or maybe I wouldn't have. I was still a child when we graduated from high school. I'm not sure I matured at university. So when you said you were going on to law school, and when you earned admittance and a scholarship to UCLA Law, I felt like you'd been given a second chance. I hadn't taken anything away from you after all.

Have I taken another chance from you, the way I took Princeton from you, by coming here? By asking you to follow me? It's so dark here I wonder whether I've dimmed your light.

I know I'm just being silly, though. Nothing could dim your beautiful light.

P.S. I've included a roll of film for you to develop. If every picture is black, it's because that's how it looks up here without you."

Ivy put the letter back in its place. She'd known her mother was smart, of course, but she hadn't known that her mother had been so smart so young. Ivy didn't feel at all capable of going to a place like Princeton, even though she was only fourteen and nearly finished with high school.

There were days, and this was one of them, that Ivy felt like her parents had named her badly. Perhaps they should have called her Minor instead of Ivy. Her friends were trapped, and here she was reading old love letters instead of trying to free them.

There's nothing wrong, Ivy thought, *and a lot right, with love letters, but things written in the past have no bearing on the present.*

Oh, how terribly mistaken she was about past love's bearing on the present! She would learn that soon, and it would be both painful and important to learn. Let us not rush things.

The Librarian had been waiting just out of sight for Ivy to finish reading the letters. It was a little creepy, but he didn't consider such things. She had finished, at least for the moment, and so when she called for him he glided in like a flying squirrel.

If she was the girl he hoped, she'd want the book on rules next. Everything was going according to plan.

"I'm finished with these for now," Ivy said. "Could

you bring me the book about the rules?"

"Of course." He handed her the book that he'd been holding already and took the pile of letters back to storage.

Let us check in on Janice and Harmwala. There is little so boring as watching someone else read a rulebook, even if it determines the fate of the party.

Neither hyenas nor giraffes have elbows. Nevertheless, the elbow room newly available to Harmwala and Janice had created an easier peace between them.

Due to Harmwala's earlier mentioned inability to eat, Janice had never been truly in danger from Harmwala's fangs. To be honest, the threat was more credible in the opposite direction: Janice had dentition well-suited to rend Harmwala's inky bits and masticate her into oblivion. Luckily, it wasn't in his nature.

But if we didn't bluster, then who would know how ferocious we would be if necessary? We must strut and fret our hour upon the stage, as the saying goes. It is not bad as advice for a guitarist, but our two friends here were finding it rather more pleasant to simply chat from opposite sides of one of the many doorways of the Library.

"Ivy will get us out of here," Janice said.

"Are you really eager to return to the mural? I feel disloyal for saying it, but I would rather stay here."

Janice rested his head on the top of the doorway and thought for a bit. "I suppose I would, too, if it wouldn't bother Ivy so much. We are her oldest friends, though."

Oldest friends? That perfidious scoundrel! May his neck be mistaken for a sausage!

Ahem. Sorry. That was terribly unprofessional of me.

Fred might have disagreed with this assessment, but he was dead and didn't count anymore. Harmwala replied. She could do that, not being dead.

"Do you think there's a way she could just stay forever? It's not like she has much of a life there. Not since Henry and Grace stopped coming home."

"Died, Harmwala. They died."

The old hyena picked with her claw at a seam in the wallpaper. She didn't like thinking about all the nights that Ivy had cried herself to sleep after the accident. Harmwala had seen several owners come and go, but Ivy was special. The residents of the mural had known her since she was a newborn. "I know. Nothing should die."

Janice laughed at that.

"A hyena lamenting death?" He stopped laughing when he saw that Harmwala was truly upset.

"Crazy, right?" A hyena tittering escaped, but Harmwala's heart wasn't in it. In the couple of days since they'd come into the Library, Harmwala had felt herself unspooling. Stories she hadn't known about herself kept trying to be told.

If they'd had more time, a few years perhaps, sitting across this doorway from one another to talk about things, they'd have known how much they agreed on. Habitual threats and fears poison the soil. Take it away, and so many things can blossom—hope, forgiveness, understanding, love.

Time hadn't stopped elsewhere, though. Ivy had nearly finished the first section of the book.

Himitsu had returned from the store.

The door opened, and he strode in, sword in one hand and doll in the other. Moe followed after him.

She waved to Janice and Harmwala as fellow companions. Seeing someone else accompanying a human, they called her over to talk. The Librarian was coming down the hallway, and it was best to make themselves scarce.

The Librarian wasn't interested in them. He was headed straight to Himitsu.

Chapter Eleven

Like many avid readers, Ivy directed all of her senses into the act of reading—eyes on the words, fingertips tracing out her thoughts on the paper or table or the arms of her chair. She did not usually stick her tongue out to let the tip of it taste the change wrought in the air by the words she was digesting, but she would not have been embarrassed to do so. There is no shame in being captured by a good book.

Fortunately for our story, Ivy had reached the end of the chapter, which described the arcane procedures by which typo-fixing amendments could be suggested by the reading public for later introduction to the rules, when she heard an unfamiliar voice a few aisles over. It was Himitsu talking with the Librarian. The Librarian was explaining some extra rules of the Library, which Himitsu must have broken.

Ivy decided to investigate. Even though the Librarian had mentioned other patrons, Ivy hadn't met any, which seemed odd to her. Libraries are busy places, and this Library was among the best she'd seen.

When Ivy came around the corner, she saw the Librarian gulping down Himitsu's phone. Had her own face looked like his, like a friend had just been murdered in front of her?

She fervently hoped not. She wasn't hooked on touchscreen games and social media. Was she? No, no, of course not. She could stop at any time. In fact, she'd been so tired after her day buying gloves that she hadn't even remembered to ask for her phone back. These days, her phone was mostly used to relieve her boredom, not to message with other people, and she hadn't been bored since entering the Library.

Himitsu recovered from his shock quickly and then experienced another. The girl in front of him (Ivy, of course, but he did not know that) had arrived as quietly as a ninja, black gloves on her hands and white gloves on her lap, only the whirring of insect wings from wheel tread on wood to announce her.

Bold Himitsu, sword in hand, anger riled by the confiscation of his phone, suspicion piqued by Moe's increasingly dire warnings, flinched. His sword clattered to the floor, and in his effort to catch the sword he scratched his thumb, bobbled the doll, grasped at it desperately, scooped it into his arms, and put his thumb to his mouth to stop the bleeding.

Bold Himitsu, doll hugged tight to him, sucking his thumb, looked sheepishly at Ivy.

"Hello," he said, in English.

"Hello," Ivy said.

"How are you?"

"I'm fine. How are you?"

"I'm fine, too. Nice to meet you!"

Himitsu was not ordinarily one to speak in exclamation-marked sentences unless he was angry, but he had not expected the conversation to go so well. Every elementary student in Japan is taught this introductory English conversation, to be applied to any context in which the other person is not clearly Japanese.

Often, this does not work out. Where Japanese is a language of expectation, of patterns and forms, with points marked for transition into new patterns, English is a language of surprise. The majority of people in the world do not speak English, despite what Himitsu thought. In this case, of course, he had gotten lucky.

Having exhausted his English, Himitsu waited. He had said the last words, his reasoning went, and so it was Ivy's turn to say something. If they didn't take turns, it would be difficult to remember who was speaking.

Traditional librarians do not approve of speaking in the library, not even when one is meeting a soul mate. The chief reason for this is not well-remembered because the advent of metal movable type in Korea and its more famous re-invention in Germany a couple of centuries later had mostly quieted the books.

Illuminated books and scrolls and palimpsests and clay tablets had given way almost entirely to printed books and typed papers, and these new documents did not complain to their librarians so bitterly. More importantly, they did not listen so keenly and could not betray secrets so freely. Their senses were now embodied in the movable type of the presses, not the mark left by the scribe's pen.

The Librarian, forged and reforged from the metals of the world's printing presses, typewriters, and lately from plastics used in printers (the source of the film covering him, which he was not yet fond of), *did* know why silence had been promoted in libraries.

Not only did he know, Himitsu had wound him only moments ago, and so some of the boy's impatience had imbued him with fresh exasperation.

"Oh for the love of books, will you just introduce yourselves to each other? Speak your own language, and see what happens!"

Ivy and Himitsu both looked at the Librarian in surprise. The Librarian looked at himself in surprise. Upon reflection, the Librarian decided that he had perhaps taken in too much change in the last couple of days. But the man upstairs had been quite specific, and had demonstrated that the rules permitted this.

Ivy went first, which relieved Himitsu. He had gone first before so it was only fair that she do so this time.

"I'm Ivy," she said, stating the obvious. "My parents

died in a car crash, and I blame myself for it. I've been hiding since then, afraid what will happen if I admit it."

She put her hand over her mouth, but it was too late. The truth had escaped it. The Librarian had demanded that they introduce themselves, and she had done so, no taking it back.

"I'm Himitsu," he said. He spoke Japanese, but Ivy understood him perfectly. Libraries are places that build understanding, and this Library simply built it more quickly. "My father had an accident with a train. I think he was trying to escape the disappointment he felt in me for failing my high school entrance exam. My friend Kenji told me it's what weak men do when they have weak sons. I've been hiding in my room since then, afraid what will happen if I admit it."

He bowed.

Ivy wheeled herself over to him, and offered her hand. Himitsu looked at this little girl in front of him in her wheelchair and felt sad for her. She had lost both parents, and couldn't even walk. Because he was feeling sorry for her, he reached his own hand out to shake, delicately so he wouldn't hurt her.

Ivy didn't know any of these thoughts. She simply saw a boy, not much older than her, with neglected strength in his arms and unvoiced pain in his eyes. She grabbed his hand and shook it.

She didn't mean to grind his bones together. It's

just that Ivy was no weakling. She'd never had an electric chair, and now one would only slow her down. Years of Ivy racing around combined with Himitsu's lack of exercise during isolation had left Ivy's hands and arms stronger than Himitsu's.

This could have been an embarrassing moment between them. Fortunately, the Librarian proceeded to explain about the library card to Himitsu, and then to give him his tasks for obtaining one.

———

While Ivy and Himitsu were making awkward faces at one another and misunderstanding each other because of superficial differences, Moe talked with Janice and Harmwala.

For reasons beyond the animals' control, Moe found them flat: two-dimensional and not actually that interesting, even though they were much larger and older than her. Moe found herself in quite a bad mood, in fact, and increasingly worried.

She checked her battery levels several times, but nothing untoward seemed to be happening on that front. As nearly as she could tell, she was still thinking, and therefore she still existed. But how does one know that one is really thinking?

Aside from calling one's self "one," of course. This has its own equivalent in Japanese, but Moe does not actually think in Japanese. It is simply a layer on top of the Universal Grammar of her thought. In the universal grammar, Moe calls herself "Self."

Self was perturbed. No word had ever been heard back from any electronic friends who had entered the Library. Why not?

She checked her communications and found that she had no wireless access to anything outside the Library. She detected nothing in the Library either, but a quick diagnostic check showed her it was nothing wrong with *her*.

The Library must form a Faraday cage. Such cages can lock up electrical signals, preventing them from entering or exiting. Well, that was fine. She would simply leave and relay a report.

Several times, she started walking toward the door. It wasn't even closed. Several times, she found herself drifting away, toward the giraffe or toward the hyena, confused.

Self, what are you doing?

She asked herself, but no answers were forthcoming.

There are many benefits to being an electronic friend, and only a few drawbacks. One of the most underrated benefits is that one can program one's Self. Moe programmed her Self to walk straight ahead until given an order to stop, and then turned her thoughts off for exactly one minute but left her camera running.

If something was interfering with her thinking, this would allow her to nevertheless keep on walking and exit the Library.

After a minute, she woke to find her body face

down, thrashing its legs against the floor. She was no nearer the doorway than she had been before. A review of the video showed her vision abruptly skew, meaning she had turned aside, and then the rapid approach of the floor when she fell.

Later models did not have her defect, but Moe, to her great shame, could not stand up if she was lying face down. She tried for a bit to wobble herself over onto her back. If she could get there, then standing up was simple.

After a few attempts, she admitted defeat. Not knowing when she could charge herself again, it was best not to waste energy on pride.

"Help! Help! I've fallen and I can't get up!"

She called it out in Japanese, and when Himitsu ignored her—or didn't hear her, but it feels the same to the one who needs attention—she called it out in English, too. Moe was not picky about what language she spoke. When you have to translate everything you say, you simply pick whichever language expresses it best.

Ivy heard her and came over to help. Moe was able to use Ivy's footrest as a brace to pull herself upright. She stood and smoothed her skirt, which had been ruffled by her ordeal.

The Librarian walked away, and Himitsu came over to see what the fuss was about.

"Are you okay, Moe-chan?"

"Yes. No thanks to you. This girl helped me."

And then it was another round of introductions, each of the children to the other's imaginary friends.

"Himitsu-kun, I'm stuck," Moe said. "I've tried leaving the Library, and I can't. I'm cut off from my server, and I don't even know how I'll recharge."

Ivy hadn't noticed the absence of electrical outlets. She wasn't a Luddite, and she used a phone, obviously, but that was the entirety of her electronic life. Her wheelchair required no power but her hands and arms, her books required nothing but sunlight to read them, and her mind could usually stimulate itself.

Himitsu, in contrast, looked around in growing horror. To him, the Library was positively barbaric in its lack of electrical outlets. Where could he plug in his tablet, his game consoles, his electric socks, his abdomen exerciser, his drink chiller? Where could he plug in his Moe? What kind of library was this, anyway? He hadn't seen a single computer.

Ivy, who had just finished reading for this very reason, explained to the friends and to us.

"The reason none of you can leave," she said, "is that by entering the Library you have agreed to the terms and conditions. Under those terms, you've agreed that the Library gets to maintain a permanent copy of your story."

Janice trumpeted his outrage. "Well that's not fair at all! I saw the agreement before I came in, but nobody reads those things."

"I, too, saw it and simply accepted," Moe said. "No

matter what it said, I would follow my friend."

Harmwala would not admit to being able to read, even though Janice had, more than once over the years, caught her perusing Henry and Grace's books, and later Ivy's.

Moe asked the relevant question. "So why does that stop us from leaving, but not you?"

"Himitsu and I, we are not our stories," Ivy said. She was wrong about this. We are the stories that we tell ourselves. But she was not too much wrong. There is a part of each person that is more author than story.

"But," she continued, "all of you are pure story. Without it, you don't exist. The Library thinks you are trying to remove its copy. There's no malice in what it's doing, but there's also no exception to allow you to leave."

That got Harmwala's attention.

"So we're stuck here forever? I've been enjoying the space, but I don't know that I want to be here forever." No matter how large, a place you cannot leave is a prison. Keeping this in mind, do not stare too long into the sky. Do not try too hard to jump. Icarus learned the hard way.

Ivy was clever enough that she knew there was a way around. Not an exception, per se, more a way to fulfill the terms of the agreement that the friends had made.

"Not forever. We need to make a copy of your stories. Then we can archive that in the Library, and you can leave. But first, Himitsu and I have to go do his tasks so he can get a library card. After that, we'll go see the copy scribe."

Chapter Twelve

Ivy's first task had been to perform a small kindness for the strangers who had been the proximate cause of her parents' death. Himitsu's first task had nothing to do with the death of his father. At least not directly. Everything is related if you take a long enough view.

He was to go "declare himself" to Yugao. Ivy had heard this part, but it wasn't clear to her quite what it meant. Efforts to clarify it with Himitsu had embarrassed him deeply.

Finally, he blurted at Ivy, "I must tell her my feelings. My love." He felt that the Librarian was picking on him, which made him angry. Despite that, perhaps it *was* time to go and declare his feelings. Moe had encouraged him to do it, and it would quiet these confused thoughts about Ivy. It had been a couple of years since he'd talked with a girl, and she was overwhelming in some ways.

He would rather have left Ivy behind. Her presence would complicate things greatly. Of course there are some people in wheelchairs in Japan, but there are few people who are visibly foreign, and fewer of them who are not young and whole, or visibly tourists. She would stick out, and she would not have a passport and stamp to show that she had arrived in Japan by conventional means.

Ivy could be confined by the police for as much as three weeks simply for being there, and they could torment her until she signed a confession written in Japanese. Himitsu knew none of this, though, so it wasn't part of his worries.

He would rather have left Ivy behind, but the Librarian told him that she must go, too, and promised that she would not cause any trouble with the police. So, Ivy behind him, Himitsu stepped through the door into his apartment, carrying his sword but leaving Moe in the Library with a dwindling battery charge and little hope of escaping before she was entirely depleted. The last he looked back, she had slumped against a wall and entered a low-power mode in which she could see and talk but not move.

When he emerged into his apartment, the sky was the dark of early evening, and he heard his mother snoring with the peace of someone whose final obligations have been met. He had been gone longer than he thought. Himitsu and Ivy found that they could no longer speak to each other, except in his halting English, but that was enough for him to ask permission and her to give it before he carefully eased her down the stairs.

Of course Himitsu still knew where Yugao lived. One of the reasons that he had fallen in love with her, or at least he had called it that, was that she lived close enough for them to fantasize about running away together. Not an elopement, but two friends headed out to adventure, to perhaps catch small monsters and battle new and exciting rivals. Children's dreams.

Ivy had no trouble keeping up with Himitsu as he jogged down the street. She didn't know how to mention it, but she could have gone much faster. He could have, as well, but not without starting to sweat. If he was going to show up in the early evening and declare himself to the girl he'd abandoned two years ago, carrying a sword and accompanied by a foreign girl in a wheelchair, he didn't want to also be sweaty.

Three blocks north and two blocks west, a knight's move from his apartment, they arrived at the street where Yugao lived. He didn't say anything, might not have said anything even if he'd known how, but Ivy hung back anyway. She could tell this was something scary for Himitsu. She did him the favor of motioning to his sword, which he handed over for safekeeping. If he needed it to talk with Yugao, things had changed beyond comprehension.

Ivy had to be content with watching him from a few houses down. In spring, a profusion of flowers would festoon the trellises along this street, housing friendly bees and unfriendly but harmless cats. At this time of year, though, Ivy saw only one flower, a large white bloom open to the night, lonely on the fence outside of Yugao's house. We can get closer.

Himitsu rang the doorbell and stepped away, stood in the street instead of on the porch, next to the gardening slippers and gloves. If nobody answered, would his task still be complete? If he walked away now, would the Librarian know he was lying?

Yugao's mother answered, the surprise obvious on her face, though she took care to hide it quickly. Some in the neighborhood said that Yugao's mother was descended from royalty, but nobody much cared about minor royalty in Nagoya unless the name was Toyoda, Mitsubishi, or one of the other names that meant Money. Royal or not, she was a portrait of decorum.

She invited Himitsu inside, but he felt too much shame to go in. There had been a time when he was a regular guest in their home, before years had passed. He might as well be a ghost for all of the contact he had kept. Even online, he had retreated from the world and those he'd known.

Yugao emerged. In the two years since he had seen her, she had grown from fourteen to sixteen. An adult might see little difference, but to Himitsu it seemed an eternity. In his own mind, he was still fourteen, still Ivy's age. He didn't spend time looking at himself in a mirror, and without anyone around him to show him slow aging, his mind hadn't caught up with the changes to his own body.

She was even more beautiful than he had prepared for her to be. In the moonlight, her skin looked like flower petals, and Himitsu noted, not without blushing, that she was blooming in a way she hadn't been two years ago.

"Long time no see. I guess you're not dead," she said.

Himitsu stammered. "Long time no see. I'm sorry I've been away for so long."

"You hurt me, you know."

"I couldn't face you, or anyone."

"Whatever. I used to feel sorry for you, but I don't know what to feel now. I don't even know who you are anymore. What are you doing here?"

The idea of telling her that he loved her, of declaring his heart, seemed ridiculous to Himitsu now. He didn't even know this young woman who stood before him. But he wanted the library card, partly because it would get him closer to understanding his father and partly because he had wound the Librarian, been affected by the magic of that act. And there was Moe, of course.

"I wanted to declare my heart," he said, "for so long. But I never did, and now you are someone different, and I am someone different. So I am here to declare something different. I have been a terrible friend, not only to you but to so many people. I am going in pursuit of truth and resolution, and so I am here to say goodbye, for now. I should have said it to you before. I hope your future is good."

He turned to go, but Yugao had never given up hope that he would emerge one day. Some young people in Japan date during high school, but it is not unusual for a girl, even a pretty girl like Yugao, to not have a boyfriend. Preparation for the university exam and participation in club life can take up all of one's time.

She grabbed him by the shoulders, leaned in and kissed him quickly on the mouth, then stepped away.

"That wasn't me, and that kiss wasn't for you," she said. "That was the girl you left behind when you retreated. Kissing the boy who didn't retreat. Come back soon, Jirou. I am happy to see you. I hope you will join a club and come be my friend again."

She turned and walked back into her house. It's traditional to turn and bow to a guest who is leaving, but she went straight to her room. Her mother, who had once been a broken-hearted girl herself, bowed to Himitsu and shut the door.

Ivy watched the tableau in front of her with mixed emotions. She hadn't heard what they'd said, and wouldn't have understood if she had. But she'd understood the bewildered look on Himitsu's face as he came back to her. Sadness at wasted time. The regret of knowing that a nectar spilled by clumsiness would have been sweet.

Ivy squeezed his hand when he retrieved his sword. She wasn't sure whether she ought to hold his hand as they made their way back to his apartment. Would that

122

be something a friend would do? Was that all she wanted? He was handsome, but she found the idea of him as a boyfriend repulsive. For once, she was glad that wheeling herself along meant she didn't have a hand to spare.

———

The rattlebump of Ivy going down the stairs had not been noisy. In a pinch, she could even navigate herself down a flight of stairs when it was not dark, though she would have been worried about the pitch of the Japanese stairs, which was different than the pitch used in Fairbanks.

Going up a flight was another matter entirely, and so she had to trust Himitsu to help her. He could have carried her to the top in his arms, borne her over the threshold of his apartment and sat her on his mother's couch while he went to retrieve the chair. Perhaps if they'd been able to converse normally, he would have suggested it. But so fresh on the heels of Yugao's kiss, unable to express himself clearly in any language, Himitsu settled for using the handles on the back of Ivy's chair to help her up the steps, one at a time.

By the time that the two of them were at his doorway, the noise they'd made had woken his mother, who greeted them both.

"Where are you from?" she asked of Ivy.

"America," Ivy said. For once, she was glad that it was a reasonable question. It was not the same as when she was questioned at home. At home, they meant "what place do you belong to, with your too dark too light skin? Who claims you as theirs? How far down do I need to look to see your place?"

"I will put on some tea," Eri said. "Welcome to our home." She bowed.

Himitsu was flustered, which was becoming distressingly normal.

"You speak English?" he asked his mother.

"Of course," she said. "Wasn't I the one who always helped you with your English homework? And how did you think I sold my dolls to America without English?"

The water was hot, and she poured. Ivy chose an orange herbal tea from the box of flavors and accepted a pair of cookies.

"Sit. Sit," Himitsu's mother told him. He sat. What followed was a rapid back-and-forth of English that Himitsu couldn't follow at all. Why hadn't his mother taken a better job, if she could speak English? In Tokyo, even waitresses were likely to speak English. In Nagoya, it was a rarer skill. Even an old woman who spoke both could find work. But then, who would have taken care of him?

"I'm fourteen," Ivy was saying. "But I'm almost finished with high school. Just another eighteen months, and then I'll go to college. But Himitsu is probably close to being done, too, isn't he?"

Himitsu's mother rolled her eyes at him, an exaggeration meant for Ivy's understanding. "Why do you lie to everyone about your name?"

He shrugged. "It's easier than explaining that you named me Jirou for no reason."

"But she wouldn't even know what Jirou means, would she? To her, it is just another Japanese name."

"I don't like my name. That's all. I don't understand why you gave it to me."

She looked unhappy at this statement, the way that she always did when he brought it up. And, just like always, she didn't explain it to him, and he didn't ask directly. In his heart, he knew he'd had an older brother, one he had no memory of.

The rice cooker beeped to indicate it was finished, and his mother served rice to the three of them. Even though it was only rice, the smell of it made Himitsu realize how hungry he was.

He rummaged through the cupboards and brought a fork for Ivy, who, as a foreigner, couldn't be expected to know how to use chopsticks. To his surprise, she was already eating when he turned back around, chopsticks in her hand being put to good use. How much else had his friends online been wrong about?

After they ate, Ivy, having always been polite where Himitsu was surly, carried the dishes to the sink and would have washed them if he hadn't intervened. He washed them himself, just so he wouldn't look bad in front of Ivy.

Behind him, his mother giggled, but silently. This

girl would be good for him, if he'd give her a chance.

When the dishes were done, Himitsu watched as Ivy hugged his mother. Feeling lonely, he got a hug from his mom, too. Then he and Ivy went back through the Library door.

Moe was lying on the wooden floor a few feet inside the doorway, limp and unmoving. Worse than that, she didn't respond to Himitsu's greetings. Janice began crying in relief when the adventurers returned. Surely they would fix this.

Chapter Thirteen

Moe's thoughts at this time are nothing to write home, or elsewhere, about. Janice was a bundle of worry, his usual state. Ivy and Himitsu had their own concerns about Moe, a mix of guilt and worry.

Harmwala was, for once, the one thinking most clearly. She didn't have broad faith in humans the way Janice did, but she'd witnessed Ivy doing difficult things before. Still, being without faith doesn't mean being without hope. Harmwala had *informed hope* that Ivy would find a way to revive Moe.

Ivy called for the Librarian. Harmwala didn't think this was the best plan. The Librarian's motives were still unclear. If this were Grace being called, she would have heartily approved, but even Grace had been skeptical of calling in the authorities. Knowing that details of her story would be exposed in the telling of it (necessary for escaping from the Library), Harmwala had been turning the tale over in her mind. Grace was a large part of it. Was it Harmwala's to tell, even to escape? If nobody else's story is part of your own, it's not really much of a story, is it?

But Grace was years dead, and Ivy would find out much of the past anyway. We'll leave Harmwala to wrestle with the problem of disclosure and how much is owed to the dead. I'll tell it to you as I saw it and spare Harmwala from the pressure to decide.

———

The two of them, Grace and Harmwala, had not really gotten along well at first. Grace yelled at Harmwala a lot during the Bad Time before Ivy's birth.

"It's fine," Grace had snapped during their worst fight, in a way that indicated it wasn't at all fine, "for you to be all sharp teeth and threats of eating, but humans aren't hyenas. I can't just tear out the throats of my enemies."

"And so you lie here waiting, like *prey*, to be relieved of the burden of your life? Get up, woman. You are an avocado, you know how to fight."

"Attorney, Harmwala. I know it's the same in French, but they're different in English."

Harmwala pretended the slip had been intentional. "Are they? Then get up off the couch and show me you are not an oily green fruit!"

Grace threw her hands up in exasperation. Harmwala knew it was exasperation, because Grace had told her what the gesture meant. "You don't understand. How could you possibly understand? I'm hurt, and you should just leave me alone. Everyone should just leave me alone. We should never have come here."

"And I belong in the jungle? Maybe you shouldn't have come here, but here is where you are."

Grace checked the phone to make sure it wasn't broken. It hadn't been any of the times she'd checked. It was 7:06 at night, and it hadn't rung all day.

"Janice," Grace called out, "tell Harmwala to shut up. Maybe she'll listen to you."

Janice looked down at Harmwala's face, and Harmwala looked up at Janice, stretched her jaws to allow the giraffe a better look at her maw.

"I'm staying out of this," Janice said. "I think you should call the police and tell them you're hurt. But tell Fred to talk to Harmwala. She won't eat him."

Let me interject that this last statement by Janice was a dubious proposition. There was no evidence that Harmwala would not, in fact, eat the noble Fred if he crossed her. Thankfully, nobody pursued that course of action.

"I can't call the police, Janice. This isn't the kind of thing you just call them about. What would they do about it? I'd be just another angry black woman, complaining to them about hurts I suffered silently in the past from white men. They'd demand to know what changed, why I waited, who I wanted to hurt. And then they'd do nothing."

"They'd do nothing," Harmwala agreed. "Sometimes there's only one choice to be made. Claws or teeth. Claws or teeth."

Grace swallowed another handful of something and drank the last of the wine. "I'm going to go take a shower, nobody follow me."

Harmwala sniffed disdainfully. As if. None of them had ever followed her. The mural didn't extend that far. "You take far too many showers, Grace. It's not healthy for a body to be so clean. And what if the phone rings?"

"I'll hear it. He'll let it ring long enough for me to get it."

It was 9:32 at night, and the phone was ringing. Grace lay on the couch, out of view of the mural, and didn't get up to answer it.

The sun came and went, came and went, and on the third day, Grace rose. She came to her feet and went to vomit in the toilet.

We heard the sound of her water and then her yelling "Poop!" More or less. Seven months later, Ivy arrived.

Grace and Harmwala had a lot of boring conversations about what it meant to be a woman men feared and wanted to tear down. They became the best of friends, and neither of them ever told Henry about that night.

Harmwala reasoned that if Grace could rise after three days and roll back the stone from her heart to welcome Ivy in, then Moe's chances were pretty good to be cared about enough to matter.

———

Meanwhile, back in the Library, Ivy asked to see the copy scribe.

"You are permitted," the Librarian said, "but the young man does not yet have a card. He cannot accompany you."

"Moe is hurt, you have to let us go see the scribe!" Ivy knew from her research into how the Library functioned that the scribe could repair the story of any of the imaginary friends while they were in the Library. The scribe could set that story back on the path it was meant to take, or transfer the narrative from one object to another. If only Fred could be brought there somehow!

"As I said, I can let you go. I cannot let him go."

"But I don't know Moe's story. I can't tell it."

"He must have a library card before he can go. He's only done half of the necessary things."

"Fine, what else does he have to do?"

Himitsu was following this exchange half-heartedly, but mostly he was hugging Moe's limp body to him, wishing he had never brought her here. Couldn't he have come alone? What kind of coward was he, that he had endangered his only friend? The pot of anger that simmered in him all of the time was threatening to boil over, to burn him again with self-hatred. "I'll do anything. I don't care. Do I have to kill someone? Because I will."

"Calm down!" Ivy shouted at him. His lack of calm was affecting her, and she was losing patience with him.

The Librarian tut-tutted at Himitsu. "Master Hayashi, I have never asked for a murder, and I never will. That is quite simply out of the question. Since you seem eager to accomplish your second task, I give it to you now. Go and speak to Kenji. It does not matter what you say, but you are not permitted to hit him, no matter what. Not with your fists and not with your sword. Is that clear? Once you've done that, return, and I will give you your card."

"I will not!" Himitsu brandished his sword one-handed at the Librarian, who did not flinch.

Ivy was deeply upset by this. Of course, even ordinary people are often bothered by violence or the threat of it. The human body has a fine sense of danger and will respond with a surge of energy to allow one to either flee the danger or face it head on. Ivy was more attuned to this sense than most people, and so although she was more cheerful than might be expected of a near-friendless orphan, she was also more prone to upset in the face of anger. "Himitsu, listen to me," she implored.

"You don't know everything Kenji did."

"Is it worth Moe's life?"

"I'll take her body with me and charge her at home. She'll be just fine after I plug her in for a while. Give me my phone back, Librarian."

The Librarian looked to Ivy, as though she could intercede further. Seeing her make no move to stop Himitsu, the Librarian retrieved the phone (let us just say that hinges and flaps can be hidden in the most typical of places) and returned it.

Himitsu strode to the door that led back into his apartment. In his heart, he suspected things were not going to be this easy. Surely the Librarian wouldn't just let him carry Moe away like this? Wasn't it supposed to be against the rules?

The giraffe and the hyena both backed away from the egress, and Himitsu passed through it.

Himitsu did not suddenly find himself walking back into the Library. It would be a silly kind of magic to let that happen, and then you might stop believing that the things I am telling you are true.

He found himself, of course, back in his home with his precious things. His dirty clothes. His unread emails (all spam) and text messages (all notifications from online services). His video games.

The feet of the Moe body made their usual clicking sound as the magnets in the shoes engaged with the magnets in the stand. Himitsu carefully positioned the limbs to be as comfortable as possible. The charging light on the base came on, the arrow of its motion a false signal that all was well. The doll was charging.

"Son? Is that you returned?" His mother scratched at his door, and he opened it for her.

"Yes, it's me. Something is wrong with Moe, so I

brought her back. She's charging."

In his heart, Himitsu knew that this wasn't strictly true. The batteries hidden in the assembly of circuits and plastics that had constituted Moe were charging, but he might as well have been force-feeding a corpse for all the good it would do.

He was too exhausted to think straight. He was too exhausted to feel straight. Looking at his mother, he knew she could see it, too. One of the most annoying things about her was how easily she saw into his heart, even when he was ashamed.

"Mom," he said. "I'm afraid. I know Moe is still stuck in the Library. I can't feel her here at all. Ivy says she knows how to get Moe back, but I need a library card."

"Come lie down. Let me clean your ears."

Himitsu sniffed at this show of tenderness, but he was glad that Ivy wasn't here to see it. Even to him, it seemed a strange display of love. Cleaning the ears of a man she loves is something better suited to an older generation than his, even though such scenes appear in the home dramas on tv. Why had his mother chosen to be so old when she had him? Everyone else's mothers were younger, in their thirties. Their early forties at worst. He had the oldest mother of anyone he knew.

He laid his head in her lap, and she stroked his hair and gently washed the wax from his ear while she coaxed him to tell her what was bothering him.

"The Librarian says I have to talk with Kenji before I can get a card, and I have to not hit him."

"Why would you hit your friend? You've never told me what happened between the two of you. He used to be like a brother to you."

"He said dad was selfish to do what he did. That he only did it because he was disappointed in me for my high school entrance scores."

"Oh, son. That was cruel words, but have you met Kenji's older brother?"

Himitsu had not, now that he thought about it. He knew Kenji must have one: *Kenji* and *Jirou* both share the meaning of second son. "What about him?"

"He went to the forest and never came back, but they found his shoes at the start of the pathway."

"I didn't know. He didn't tell me." If you weren't going to return from the forest, it was a kindness to your family to leave your shoes at the start of the path, along with identification. The families would know not to search, not to hold out hope.

His mother kissed his forehead gently and signaled him to turn so she could access the other ear. "Sometimes we hurt the ones we have most in common with."

Jirou cried softly into his mother's lap, not even caring if she noticed. "There's one more thing, though. That wasn't all he said. He also called me half."

Half Japanese.

Half not.

Something warm and wet dropped into his ear, and he felt his mother's breath still for a moment before she resumed. She didn't say anything.

"Mother? It's not true, is it? You never cheated on dad."

"I think," she said very quietly, "that you should talk to Kenji. Fix your friend Moe. Read the letters in the Library."

"The letters? I thought it would bring Father back to life."

"In a way. Much of our life is how other people know us and remember us. It will not bring his body back. That's in ashes on the shrine. You know that."

Himitsu had known it, of course.

"But Mother? Is he right? Am I half?"

She stood up abruptly, dumping him unceremoniously to the floor. "That's an ugly word. I don't want you saying it anymore. You are wholly yourself."

She went to her room and shut the door. When Himitsu called to her, she didn't respond, even though he could hear her making a noise.

It was the sound of a mother grieving a child she's lost, a sound he'd never heard before and didn't recognize. A mother asking a daughter, once again, what had gone wrong.

Soon, it stopped, and both of them fell asleep.

Chapter Fourteen

If you listen closely, you'll hear Ivy singing to herself in the dark of the Alaskan night. She's left the door to the Library open and shifted herself to the couch so that she can hear her friends while she drifts to sleep.

Harmwala graces Ivy's song with her own. Giraffes can't sing, at least not well, but the rumble coming from Janice's humming forms a counterpoint to the melody of the other two. Giraffes are among the world's best at humming.

For Ivy, it was almost as good as having them in the room with her.

We leave them in peace, however, and join Himitsu as he sets out to confront Kenji. Because it is nighttime in Alaska, it is late afternoon in Nagoya, and everyone has already left school.

Himitsu tried, of course, to switch Moe back on, a last-ditch attempt to avoid this meeting with Kenji. When the falsely familiar voice of his friend instructed him to please register his information to teach the Schoolgirl Friend (Version Three) to recognize him, he switched the body off and found some courage deep inside himself, where it had lain neglected beneath a pile of self-pity.

The afternoon bus was no longer crowded with school kids headed home and not yet crowded with workers, so Himitsu sat by himself and waited. The city had raised the bus fare since the last time he'd ridden. He had enough money on his Manaca, the IC card for city transportation, but it frustrated him that they were always doing things like that. He didn't like these little reminders of all the time he'd lost.

When Kenji's stop came, Himitsu stayed on the bus. As it pulled away, he cursed himself for cowardice and pushed the button to signal the driver. At the next stop, he left the safety of the bus and started the walk back toward Kenji's house.

He suddenly discovered how thirsty he was and stopped to buy himself a bottle of water. Why not have some cup noodles, too? And it would be rude to walk while eating, so he sat at the lunch counter.

But finally he ran out of excuses. Too soon, and years too late, Jirou found himself at Kenji's door. He rang the bell.

Perhaps if Kenji weren't home, the Librarian would give him credit anyway. The sound of footsteps dashed that hope.

"What?" That was Kenji, being rude when he saw our friend Himitsu before him in need.

"You were wrong about my father. You were wrong about me. I'm as Japanese as you are, and he was proud of me."

Kenji snorted. "Go away, loser."

"I know about your brother. Did you disappoint him?"

It wasn't that Himitsu had never been struck before. Being struck came with the territory when taking sword lessons. But it had never come as such a surprise to him.

That is, Kenji had just punched him in the nose.

Luckily for both of them, Himitsu hadn't been ready. If he had been, he would have struck back, and then he might not get his library card. Plus, even after his long confinement he was a much better fighter than Kenji.

It's almost, Himitsu thought, *as though Kenji wants me to beat him up.*

It is said, by the people who make up things to say, that when two tigers fight, one is maimed and the other is killed. Nearly slanderous, because No True Tiger would stoop to such barbarity. More likely at least one of them was a striped lion, trying to make tigers look bad.

Occasionally, though, misunderstandings rise to such a fever pitch that someone throws a punch without quite understanding why they're so angry.

Himitsu sat on the curb with his nose bleeding.

Soon, Kenji settled down next to him.

Himitsu turned to his erstwhile friend. "Yugao

kissed me."

"Lucky you."

"I'm not half, you know. You shouldn't say I am."

Kenji rolled his shoulders forward and stared at the ground where a few drops of Himitsu's blood had fallen. "Wouldn't it be okay if you were, though?"

"No. My mom didn't cheat. And halfs are ruining the Japanese race. If we accept them, we might as well accept gays and foreigners and give up our jobs to women who are just going to get pregnant anyway."

"Jirou? That doesn't sound like you. Do you really think those things are so terrible? You really think being half is shameful?"

"It's not the worst thing to be. But I'm not. Why do you keep saying I am?"

Kenji licked his finger and tried to rub a spot from his shoe. "My parents said it. It's no wonder I turned out the way I did, hanging out with the half son of a murdering whore mother."

Himitsu gave Kenji a hard look. That kind of talk deserved a beating. There are some things you don't joke about, and this didn't sound like a joke. It didn't sound like a taunt, either. His mother hadn't said no. "You've met my mother. You know it's not true."

Kenji snorted. "Sometimes you're so thick I don't know how we became friends. That's not your mother. That's your grandmother."

Again, the urge to reach out and shut someone up before they could tell him things he didn't like nearly overwhelmed Himitsu. But this was how things had always been between him and Kenji.

Sometimes there's only one choice to make: claws or truth. "My grandmother? Are you sure?"

Kenji shrugged in the way that said yes but let Himitsu ignore it if he wanted. Friends can be kind like this.

If Himitsu had a non-Japanese parent—he already felt hurt at thinking of himself as half—then his friends online were wrong. They probably wouldn't be his friends if they knew. Some of them would have. Some of them, like Himitsu, had joined their own bullies, rather than endure them. But Himitsu didn't know this.

He looked at the friend in front of him, the one who had said such hurtful things and punched him in the face but seemed, even so, so much better than the people in the forums. There was no hate in Kenji's face, Himitsu saw.

But hurt? So much of it. In his own hurt and anger, Himitsu had kept himself secret from others. When you wall yourself away, neither side can see through. When had Kenji's nose gotten the break at its tip? Had the back of his hand always had that scar, a short thick exclamation point, the same width as an electrical cord?

Without thinking about it, Himitsu reached out and stroked it, once. He looked up at Kenji's face again.

Perhaps you'll avert your eyes or shy away, knowing

what's about to happen. Perhaps you'll skip to the end of the scene. Perhaps you won't.

Himitsu did not avert his eyes. Himitsu did not shy away. Kenji kissed him.

Not every kiss is stolen, some are given.

"This," Kenji said, gesturing to the space between them, "is me." He placed Himitsu's fingers back on the scar. "My father forbids it. So this is me, too."

"I thought... you and Yugao? You and the other girl?"

"Some people are not one thing. Maybe I'm half, in that way."

"No," Himitsu said. "That's an ugly word, and I don't want to hear you using it."

You cannot see the body language that passed between them, the give and take of motion, glance, and breath that friends use to communicate. It would take fourteen years of friendship and two years of angry distance to teach it to you. To save time, I will tell you the meaning.

Kenji knew Himitsu loved him but was not romantically interested in him. Neither of them had to say it, so neither of them did. Friends can be kind like this, too.

"I have to go," Himitsu said. "Video games, tomorrow?"

"Sure," Kenji said. They both knew it wouldn't be tomorrow. But it would be soon.

When Himitsu boarded the bus, the driver asked whether he was alright. Himitsu, who was feeling better than he had in years, didn't understand until the driver motioned to the areas that were still bloody. The clerk at the convenience store had given him wet tissue, per usual, which Himitsu used to wipe away the signs of reconciliation.

The rest of his trip home was uneventful.

A quick swipe of soapy paper was enough to get rid of the superficial evidence, but parents are not fooled by such hasty repairs. Eri knew when she saw her son that the fight with Kenji had ended. She also knew that just because a fight is over doesn't mean the hurt is gone.

"I'm home," he said.

"Welcome back, son," she said.

"Hello, grandmother," he said. Even true things can be cruel to voice.

"Do you want to talk about it?"

Himitsu shrugged at her.

"I have acted as your mother your whole life. Doesn't that give me some right?"

"What happened to my real mother?"

"Her husband died, and she kept raising her son anyway. Even when he was hurtful."

"You're talking about you. I mean my real mother. My biological mother."

"They're not the same thing. My daughter, your biological mother, was troubled."

"You mean crazy, right?"

"I mean troubled. Crazy is an easy label for things we don't understand."

"What happened? You're just saying vague things at me." He was right about this. Partly, Eri was reluctant to share the burden of knowledge with her son. The other part was that because Japanese allows being ambiguous and counting on the listener to understand, a straightforward statement can seem brutal.

"Go to the Library and read it for yourself. Without context, you will misunderstand."

"And how do you know so much about the Library? It seems awfully convenient, and you've told me so many lies. My whole life, for one."

"After the war, there were many orphans. Some of us went there. Some of us were helped. Some of us helped, even though it hurt."

Despite his anger and confusion, Himitsu knew that his mother, the real one standing in front of him now, loved him. This knowledge did not take away his newfound hunger to know more about his birth mother, though. And why did he go to all of the trouble of seeing Kenji if he wasn't going to get his stupid library card?

And, his brain prompted him, *what about your birth father?*

Chapter Fifteen

Simon had been complaining incessantly since Ivy's departure. Elizabeth was prepared to take certain measures in response to Simon's complaints.

She wasn't upset about him complaining. A good complainer was nothing to sneeze at, by her reckoning. If you were to send someone to Iberia to be questioned, they might lie. And of course they'd act surprised, as though nobody expected it.

A complainer, in contrast, would give you all of that information for free. Often, they didn't even realize what they were saying.

"Where are you?"

When she called out, Simon stumbled back around the corner. He had been taking care of some business he thought it best the girls not see, even if they could still smell it. Probably they couldn't smell it.

"Lizzie, Lizzie! What you want?" His words were only a little slurred.

"Do you think we could visit the Library sometime?"

"You don't want to do that! You'd just get stuck. There's probably hundreds of folks like you stuck in there. Thousands, for all I know."

"Who leads them?"

"Huh? Nobody. They're just there."

Knowing that there were hundreds, perhaps thousands, of subjects just waiting for leadership made Elizabeth very sad indeed. From Simon's complaints, she had suspected this was the case. It simply could not be allowed to continue.

"You must open the door again. We must rescue them!"

"It's too late for them. Forget about them."

Simon couldn't seem to take his own advice, though. When he slept, his dreams were filled with his friends, screaming and running from fire. He'd been promised the flames would set everyone free, but instead there'd just been the screaming and the sirens and the loneliness after. Even his brother had abandoned him.

Elizabeth needled at Simon for hours, until she finally bored him into it. He drew the door where the dust of the one Ivy had come through still lurked. He wrote the words, and stood back as the door opened.

When Elizabeth ran through the door, Simon staggered after her. In his haze, which had retreated (but not far enough) over the hours since his last indulgence, Simon didn't wonder where Mary had been. Usually she was so close.

He heard her, as he crossed the threshold, screaming his name. To him, it sounded as though she were getting louder, but she was just getting closer.

Mary poked her head through the door, and Elizabeth, who had been waiting for just this moment, slammed it shut.

Mary's head popped off and rolled down along the baseboards before coming to rest on the remnant of neck near a particularly lovely fleur-de-lis stenciled on one of the bookshelves.

"That was really uncalled for," Mary said. She looked up (as though she had a choice) at Elizabeth with resentment.

"If it was good enough for my mother, it's good enough for you." Elizabeth smirked.

Something didn't seem quite right to Elizabeth, though.

"Simon, where are we? What's wrong with these books? I can't figure out any of the titles."

Even though Simon was in low spirits and just wanted to sleep—he could see a striped chaise not too far away that would be heavenly to collapse onto—he looked at the bookshelf.

"Nothing wrong with it," he said. "You can't read it 'cause it's French subjects."

That wouldn't do at all. You couldn't trust French subjects. Elizabeth stalked off to find some good English ones.

"I'm not sure I'll miss her," Mary said, "but maybe we should stop her."

———

Reluctantly, Simon resisted the siren's call of the chaise. Mary's head couldn't simply be picked up. Even without her body attached, it was still, after all, only a smattering of paint.

"Alright, alright," Simon muttered to himself even though nobody had asked him a question. He took some chalk from his pocket and drew a thick horizontal line just below Mary's neck and a hardhat on her head.

"Did you just draw me a pedestal and a snake that has swallowed an elephant?"

"It's a helmet. In case you bump your head. That's a spring below you. Try jumping."

Mary tried jumping, and with a sproinging sound discovered that she could bounce herself around without too much trouble. Without arms to stabilize her, she soon discovered Simon's wisdom in drawing something to protect her head.

The clack and clatter of Mary bounding into lintels and doorframes and bookshelves soon attracted the attention of the Librarian, who had not been expecting them. At least, not so soon.

He strolled into view. "I do hope you're not here to cause trouble, Simon."

You might find it odd that Simon had kept his library card for these many years. Even after he'd lost his driver's license (revoked for good cause), his Social Security card (stolen), and his dignity (to be recovered at a later date), he'd managed to hang onto the card from so many years earlier. He pulled it out now and brandished it at the Librarian.

"I'm allowed to be here. You said. I just had to do those things, and I could come here when I wanted."

"You haven't wound me in many years, though. And you certainly haven't talked with me every day."

"That was never what you said. You said you'd leave if I didn't do that, not that I couldn't find you. Sometimes people leave. Always people leave. That's got nothing to do with me. If you didn't want to be found again, you shouldn't have interfered by sending that spy."

"Ivy," the Librarian supplied.

"Sure, Ivy. You should have left her out of it. Why not send Sandra?"

"You know very well why Sandra didn't come."

And Simon did know. He had broken the wrong rules after being admitted to the Library that first time. The infraction hadn't warranted revocation of the library card—few rules were that important—but it had resulted in suspension of delivery services.

Mary had been observing this interaction with interest. Like most characters, she found it difficult to talk with more than one person at a time, but now she felt compelled to notify Simon and the Librarian of something important.

"While you two are reminiscing, Elizabeth is off doing who knows what to who knows whom. Do you smell smoke?"

They did.

Simon and the Librarian ran to see what was going on. Mary was as interested as they were, but she was completely unconcerned with keeping pace. Whenever they got there, she would be a head.

Simon arrived first, but seeing the shelves on fire reminded him too much of what had happened to him, what had given him access to the Library in the first place, and he retreated to where he couldn't see the flames. He put his hands over his ears to block out the crackling sound. Surely the Librarian would put it out, and he could be spared the vision.

Though it had been his intent only to flee, not to keep himself out of the way of the Librarian's firefighting efforts, Simon's departure allowed the fire suppression system to be safely activated. Inert gases flooded the burning area, and soon the fire went out.

Elizabeth, peeping from around the corner to see how things were going, was disappointed at how little her efforts had achieved. "I'll just do it again!" she shouted to them, "and nothing you can do will stop me."

The Librarian gave her an admonishing look. "I'm a Librarian, and this is a library. Of course I can stop you," he said. He fished around in his storage space for a bit, then pulled out a roll of tape and a pen. Working quickly, he framed Elizabeth within a square of tape and then wrote "First Class" in the corner of the square.

Elizabeth snorted at him. "As though this would stop me from going anywhere! Idiot! Moron!" She began stomping away, but the frame just followed her. No matter how she tried, she couldn't escape it, nor could she affect anything outside of the frame. "What'd you do to me?"

"I've put you in a first class stamp. It won't stop you from going anywhere. You can get just about anywhere with such a stamp. But you'll still be in the stamp. You're not the first troublemaker I've had."

Elizabeth was flattered that the Librarian thought she was first class. She still fumed and plotted. There are standards of conduct for queens, after all. Elizabeth wanted nothing so much as acknowledgment that she was a queen. The Librarian left her to it and went to check and see how Simon was doing.

Simon was not doing well. There was nothing to drink in the Library, or he would have been reaching for it. Seeing the fire, hearing the taunts, he had been pushed back to the night he'd become an orphan.

Like many people who become teachers when

they grow up, Simon had been raised with readily available books and an appreciation of the power of reading. Books were his friends, "cold but sure," as Victor Hugo had written. Simon hadn't had many other friends. That had been alright. Sometimes he'd drawn them for himself, or drawn himself a dog, but after a while he usually got bored of them.

His mother had worked hard at her job, and his father had stayed home to take care of him. In those days, stay-at-home dads were unusual. There was a strong sense, in fact, that they were lesser men, who must be unfit providers if they let their wives go out into the world instead of them.

One night—and I tell you this only so that you don't judge Simon too harshly for who he turned out to be—Simon's father woke him up and told him they were going to play a trick on mom.

Simon helped his father splash gasoline onto the too-empty bookshelves, the too-old couch, the too-small tv, and the too-ugly rugs. All the symbols of not being enough. "Go wake your brother," his father had said. And then he had splashed gasoline on his too-angry self, gone in to lie down with his too-lovely wife, and lit them both on fire.

Simon and his brother had escaped the fire. More accurately, Simon and his brother had escaped being burnt alive by the fire. Nobody truly escapes such a thing. It is possible to heal from it, but that is not the same as escaping.

People who use metaphors to avoid ugliness talk about the beauty of the pearl, how a small irritant can cause an oyster (some other shellfishes also form pearls, but let's not be pedantic) to develop a pearl. It is rare to hear someone consider what it must be like for the oyster. To be bothered for years by something that should have been a minor irritant. To have it get worse, year-by-year, to increase in size until finally someone fatally cuts you open and removes it.

Neither Simon nor his brother was an oyster. Their pain had not grown into pearls. The wound of their parents' deaths had driven them apart. Fire had haunted Simon ever since. He saw it in his nightmares and shouted it in the streets, hoping that someone, somewhere, would show him he was wrong. The Librarian knew this.

Perhaps it was Ivy's kindness. Perhaps it was Himitsu's pain. Perhaps, even, it was some remnant of the boy that Simon had been the last time he'd wound the Librarian. Whatever it was, the Librarian stooped down and picked Simon up. He cradled Simon like a prodigal son who had returned after wasting all of himself, and whispered "It's not your fault. It was never your fault."

The Librarian knew something had to give. He'd have to push Ivy harder if things were going to work out.

Chapter Sixteen

Most nights, Ivy slept without difficulty from late evening until very early in the morning. This was helpful during both winter, when it was dark most of the day, and summer, when it was light most of the night, because she didn't depend on the sun to signal to her when to sleep. People who relied on the sun for sleep signals in Fairbanks were also known as "people who moved away from Fairbanks."

Ivy had left Himitsu and the others intending to go home and sleep for the night. Things were normally easier to figure out and more likely to be satisfactorily resolved after a good night's sleep.

Before she could sleep, Ivy had a few assignments to finish. She had agreed to stop selling her talents to university students, but the agreement had not included existing work. We know how conscientious Ivy is, and so it is unsurprising that she wanted to finish everything.

She ordered delivery pizza for dinner. This was an unusual indulgence for her. With careful budgeting, she could make the money she earned from "tutoring" last throughout the month. There were lots of bills. Heating was expensive. Light cost money. Food cost money. She didn't have much for extravagances like pizza.

The money given to her for caretaking the Library was much more than she earned from tutoring, though. When you're used to barely getting by and you suddenly have enough, it's natural to try and use it up before it's taken away. Ivy regretted not using her parents up in this way, but she hadn't known she was going to lose them.

When the pizza arrived, she paid the driver. She tipped him, too. Perhaps her tip could provide some ease in his life. As she ate, she felt increasingly sad with each bite. Her father, the times he'd been in town, had rolled out pizza dough from scratch, and they'd each decorated their own with the desired toppings and then baked them in the oven. She usually chose pepperoni and bell peppers, but sometimes she made wilder choices. Sliced apples with peanut butter. Broccoli with alfredo sauce.

Having this standardized substitute now only evoked those memories without satisfying the underlying hunger. After eating a few slices, she put the rest in the refrigerator for later, finished her work, and took herself to bed.

A few days before Sandra had shown up with the Library doors, Ivy had checked out new books from the public library. Her high school was across the street from the main library, and she was known there as a fast-reading regular. The new books seemed silly and unimportant. Why should she care about whether the girl became a vampire princess? Everyone knew these weren't real things. Vampires weren't. Princesses weren't.

They weren't real like the letters that her parents had written to each other. They weren't real like Moe and Janice and Harmwala. Like Himitsu.

How was she supposed to feel about him? He was surly and rash, and though she found him quite handsome there was something that told her she ought to stay away from romance with him. That her classmates at school were so much older only deepened her confusion. Kids in her grade were driving cars, going on dates, worrying about pregnancy.

She didn't feel ready for that. It was not even that he obviously had feelings for Yugao—Ivy had seen how shocked he'd looked after Yugao kissed him. There was something more that made it feel wrong to think of him as a potential boyfriend.

Eventually, Ivy grew frustrated with her lack of focus. She certainly wasn't sleepy, and she was no longer hungry, but she just didn't feel like reading what she had available in her house.

Giving in to the inevitable, she hoisted herself back into her chair and went back to the Library.

During some of the times that we've been following

Simon and Himitsu, Ivy had gotten to know her way a bit better around the stacks. It would have been boring to show you, since it mostly consisted of her reading the explanations of the filing system.

She went to the section where her parents' things were stored and pulled out the sheaf that contained things written near the time of her own birth.

Not at all randomly, she chose the first letter her mother had written after her birth. I would tell you that it was a heartbreaking letter, but I know you hate it when people declare what your feelings are without consulting you, so I'll let you decide about the letter for yourself.

————

My Dearest Henry,

As I write this, I am trembling with both fear and anger. How dare you! Except I know how you dare. I gave you the permission to dare when I didn't answer your calls in the time after. Couldn't you please trust me that I had good reason? Or at least trust me that I was caught as unawares by it as you were? I thought the timing would come out differently and make it not matter.

Now you've seen her, and you can count, and so you know what I've done. The girl. We must name her at some point, you know. Already she's been due a name for weeks. I thought we had decided to name her after your Nana? I still think we ought to, but I will respect your wishes in this. To a point.

She is not damaged!

If you want to call me that, I will accept the label. I have been damaged.

The girl does not deserve that label, though. Life will be hard enough for her if the doctors are right and she never gains the use of her legs. To be labeled as damaged on top, simply because of how she was conceived?

No. You are a better man than that. Get over yourself.

You will be her father. She will be your daughter. You will never speak to her of this. Not because I forbid it but because you are a better man that that, and you won't punish her for my mistake.

I know you will be her father. And I want you to come back. To be my husband again.

It is my body, so this is not your business. But you are my heart, so it is. I will explain what I couldn't at the hospital, when I was caught by surprise. I had thought that the girl would be yours in all ways. I had hoped, anyway.

Yes, I'm avoiding it. Hold your judgment. If you want to blame me after you finish reading, I can't stop you.

It was Jacob. My new boss. You've met him. It still burns to say his name. Even to write it. But you'll leave him alone, or so help me I will take the girl and we'll go. That would hurt you more than you realize yet.

With you out of town, I was the only one at

the office who didn't have someone to return home to. When Jacob asked me to work extra, to help finish some documents, it was hardly surprising. You know how hard everyone at the office works.

When he ordered food for the two of us, it seemed only right. I was doing him and the firm a favor by being there so late that I missed a reasonable time for dinner.

You know I love wine. Maybe if I had just left that alone, things would have been different. Maybe I should leave it alone now, in memory. But it's become one of my few friends. I missed it so much when I was pregnant.

If you love me, you'll stop reading the letter here and burn it. If you love me, you'll finish reading the letter and forgive me. Hold me. Never let me guess whether you finished the letter or burned it.

I led him on. That wasn't what I intended. He said his wife is dull and boring. She doesn't excite him as much as I did.

Did you know she is his second wife? He's been married before, in Japan. He mentioned it once, but never talked about it again. Had his first wife become dull and boring, and so he'd sought the second?

Here in Fairbanks, my body usually acts as armor, protecting me from the glances of the men. So many men in Alaska, but they want the white ones. I thought.

His wife slapped me once. Did you know? It was all the gossip at the office. With tears in her eyes, she reached out her hand and struck me. I deserved it.

If I hadn't worked late with him, he would've left me alone.

If I hadn't eaten with him, he wouldn't have gotten the wrong idea.

If I hadn't had the wine.

But I did. And when he told me how pretty I was and how much he hoped I had a long career and then undressed me, I didn't fight him off.

I told him I didn't want it. I swear to you I did.

But I know it wasn't enough. I didn't scream. I didn't claw.

You deserve someone so much stronger than me.

But there's this girl. And she needs a father.

There's this woman. And she needs a friend.

Please be that father.

Please be that friend.

Love, always.

———

Ivy didn't realize she was holding her breath until she became dizzy and took a deep gasping sobbing shudder of air. She had been happy. She had. That wasn't a lie. Her father had loved her. Henry was her father. Maybe he'd never read the letter, because who could know these things and love her like a daughter?

So many times, too many times, she'd gotten

frustrated with her dad for his long absences and his refusal to take things seriously. But she'd never doubted that he loved her.

She had come to the Library because she'd been feeling restless, and this letter had only made that feeling worse. Upset as she was, Ivy was careful not to damage the letter. She'd arranged the stack of papers to let her refile the letter when she was done, and so it was easy to put it back and take out the next letter. Her father's reply, dated ten days later.

———————

Consummate Grace,

I needed this time to come to terms with my rage. I wish I could tell that you I did so by sober and mature reflection or by kneeling in prayer and receiving guidance. I will not lie to you.

Last night, when the boys were drinking and playing cards, I joined them. After a few hands of cards and more than a few beers, I got into a fight with the boss's son. The words he said to provoke me don't matter. He won't be repeating them.

What matters is the rush I felt as my fist crashed into him. Here was this man, who represents everything that I want in my life, and I laid him low with one tremendous wallop. He's still going to become the boss one day, whether or not he deserves it. If I'm still working here, I'll still have to call him sir, and listen to him complain that he's got to come to the slope more than he'd like, but far less than us.

For a brief moment, I was omnipotent. I was a god with the power of death in my hands, deciding whether to spare his fragile life. He had dared to tread on me, just because he could.

I wanted his fear, and I took it from him against his will.

I know you think me not a violent man, but it is simmering always below the surface. The Bible says that the natural man is an enemy to God. I don't know whether I believe that. But the natural man is certainly an enemy to man.

I wrote above that it doesn't matter what was said. It does. He said I'd probably be working for him my whole life, now that I had a cripple kid, and should quit thinking my uppity wife would get me out of this.

Grace, I know it was wrong to hit that man. I was just so angry at what he said. Today, though, I'm grateful to him.

I am that girl's father, as much as Joseph was Jesus' father. Look at me. I guess my mama's lessons took after all.

I don't want her named after my grandmother. I loved Nana, but Eudora is the name of an old woman. I know we joked about it before, but I think we should call her Ivy.

She's going to need to be tough, and she has the world's toughest mother to learn that from. I want her to always know that she is destined to do great things, as long as she works hard to earn that destiny.

I'll be home next week, right on schedule.

You remember I'm stupid, right? I'm just warning you. I love you, and I trust you, but I'm still coming to terms with everything. I've got a lot of anger about what happened, and I'm not great at aiming it. Please be patient with me if I say something that hurts your feelings.

I see the trust in you telling me what happened, but this is new to me. I understand better now why you've been so cold. Forgive me for being frustrated with how slow and heavy things have been.

You're worth any wait. You're worth any weight.

Love, undimmed.

Chapter Seventeen

Forgiveness left Himitsu in a bad mood. It was bad enough that he had been tricked, at first, into leaving his apartment. To be made to revisit his past on top of that had been too much, and if it hadn't turned out as well as it had, with him regaining his friends and learning something true (though painful) about his mother, Himitsu would not have returned to the Library.

Except for the matter of Moe, of course. Like the first time that he'd entered the Library, Himitsu carried a sword in one hand and a limp body in the other. Unlike that first time, the body was Moe's.

How easy it was for him to forget her when faced with real people. She would not have cast him off so quickly, he knew, and it made him feel ashamed. Just because someone's body is different doesn't make them less.

"Librarian, where are you?" Himitsu shouted it into the room when he entered. It was time to get his library card, get Moe, and get out of here.

Not seeing the Librarian (who was busy dealing

with Elizabeth's tantrum and Simon's collapse), Himitsu stalked up and down the rows of shelves until he found Ivy sitting by herself at one of the reading desks.

"Ivy, where is the Librarian?"

He hadn't intended to yell. It was something that happened when he was upset or irritated, but he didn't mean anything negative by it. But he had yelled at Ivy.

She looked up at him, and he could see she'd been crying. Even to Himitsu, who barely knew her, tears looked out of place on Ivy's face, melancholy intruders. He set down his weapon, put Moe's body into a nearby chair, and then brushed Ivy's tears away with the backs of his fingers.

Ivy reached her own hands up and grabbed his. She held them lightly against her face. How long had it been since she'd had simple human touch? Most people take it for granted. Some people convince themselves they don't need it. Even the barest brush, of fingertips against a palm as a cashier hands back change, can pass the spark of humanity from person to person.

A hunger in her, a loneliness that her mind had denied but her heart had been screaming out, masking it in happy songs, spoke to a hunger in Himitsu, and he sat next to Ivy. He wrapped his arms around her. She wrapped her arms around him.

And they talked. And they cried. And they talked some more.

I'm not holding anything back from you here.

There was no kissing, no sudden making out. Even if you were hoping for it here, you'll be glad, later, that it didn't happen. It would have made things weird between them.

Even though there was no kissing, their hearts began to beat to the same rhythm. Ivy saw in Himitsu the same stubborn curve of the jawline that she saw in herself. Himitsu saw in Ivy the same ambition that had kept him relentlessly pushing forward, until the day that he'd stopped.

Each had an awkward formation in their own heart, which they'd always assumed was the universe's way of conspiring to make them sensitive. In fact, their hearts were adjoining jigsaw pieces, now locked together.

I trust you understand.

They were made for each other.

No kissing.

———

Even though the Librarian had been honestly delayed and had not intended to leave Ivy and Himitsu alone—he, too, hadn't wanted to risk them kissing—it had worked out for the best, the way that things tend to do over long enough timescales.

By the time the Librarian returned, Ivy had fallen asleep. Himitsu was wearing Ivy's gloves and reading some of Grace and Henry's letters. Ivy had picked them out for him and asked him to read them. It was easier than explaining, which tended to sound like boasting. She was proud of her parents' love for each other and wanted Himitsu to see how lucky she was to have had them as parents.

"Master Hayashi. I've brought your library card. You've earned it." The Librarian frowned at Ivy. It wasn't strictly allowed for her to give the letters to Himitsu. However, because there was no punishment specified for the infraction, he could let it pass unmentioned. It was only a technicality that Himitsu hadn't had the card yet.

Himitsu accepted the card and looked to make sure that his name was correct. He saw that it said both Himitsu and Jirou, depending on which name he thought of at the time. It wouldn't switch to other names, though. It was a real library card, not psychic paper.

He nudged Ivy gently. "Ivy, I'm sorry to wake you, but I have my library card."

She smiled at him. She'd been having the most wonderful dream, and now she woke to find that at least some of it was true.

"Let's get the others," she said.

Himitsu picked up Moe's body, and Ivy went to the wall where Janice and Harmwala were sleeping. Ordinarily, hyenas are nocturnal, and so Harmwala ought to be awake, but the mural artist had decided to make all of the animals awake at the same time, when the sun could come through the windows of the house. The habit had stuck with Harmwala. It made it easier for her to talk with Janice and the humans.

Ivy reached out and stroked the paper where their ink had gathered. If she closed her eyes, it felt like warm fur. "Wake up you guys. It's time to help Moe."

They rose without complaint and joined Himitsu and Ivy with the Librarian.

"We'd like to go to the copy scribe now," Ivy said.

"Very well." The Librarian walked across the room, taking a circuitous route that avoided the section where he'd left Simon asleep with his head cradled on an atlas of the land of Nod, and out one of the many identical doors.

Everyone followed him out. He shut the door they'd just come through and opened the next door over.

"Please. After you," he said. He motioned them in, and they entered the lair of the copy scribe.

Tigers' stripes are useful in the jungle because the alternation of light and dark mimics the dappling caused by sunlight through the trees. This lets tigers sneak up on their friends and give them a nice surprise.

In a similar way, the copy scribe had put stripes of solid and mirrored surfaces on all of the walls, which made it difficult to determine how large the room was or even to see its contents. Harmwala was suddenly in the midst of a whole clan of hyenas, each of whom was protecting her giraffe friend from the others.

"Can you tone it down somehow?" Ivy wasn't sure who was responsible for this, but she had often had good luck with asking directly for what she wanted.

The copy scribe obliged, and the mirror images faded until they were nearly transparent. Ivy saw the scribe clearly now and was surprised.

"What can we call you?" Ivy asked. Polite inquiry is often a good mask for rude surprise.

The scribe bowed. "I am Shamhat. You may call me Shamhat or the scribe. There are other names, but I see you are only children."

Shamhat stood before them, dressed in a profusion of silk. Whenever Ivy felt that she had understood what shape was hidden beneath all of the cloth, Shamhat moved, and her clothes shifted in ways that both mesmerized and confused.

Honestly, Ivy was a bit disappointed. She had imagined that the copy scribe was going to look like a giant spider, busily moving its limbs in tandem, standing on four legs and writing rapidly with the other four.

Himitsu held Moe's body out to Shamhat. "This is my friend's body. She won't wake up, and Ivy said you can probably help."

Shamhat looked sharply at the Librarian. "You told them about me?"

The Librarian, in turn, shook his head in emphatic denial. "I said nothing of the sort. I would no more break the rules than you would. But the girl," and here he pointed at Ivy, "has read the references, and she discovered your presence. I have merely brought them here at their request."

"It is good. You may go," she said to the Librarian. This seemed more like a command than permission, and the Librarian walked out the door, which closed behind him.

Shamhat took Moe's body from Himitsu and then directed him to a soft couch positioned behind a low table. Himitsu sat, and Ivy parked herself next to him.

Shamhat laid Moe's body on the table and arranged it so that Moe's feet were pointed like an accusation at Himitsu and her arms were placed with one on her chest and one stretched out to the side.

"And where is the new copy?"

Himitsu hesitated. He had the body that Moe had chosen, but he had grown accustomed to the one she'd always occupied. "You can't put her back into the same body?"

Shamhat shook her head, which set large bangles in her ears to jingling, a sound like hail on a tin roof. "Life changes a body, and you cannot ever go back to what used to be. Once a body is finished, it must be broken down into its finest parts and spread across the whole world to be reused. Some people say that we are made of stardust, and we are, but stardust cannot re-ignite the star."

Himitsu set the doll down, placing it in the same pose as Moe's body but with its hand holding hers. Shamhat nodded in approval.

"Now," she said, "you must tell me about her. I will draw the wild feelings from your heart and tame them, push them into this body where they can take root and grow wild again.”

“Moe was my friend,” he said. “She liked to go to Ueno park, and she wanted to be a pop idol.”

Shamhat struck, quick as an adder, and slapped Himitsu in the face three times, yelling at each strike. “No! Liar! You do not deserve her back!”

Himitsu rose, anger in his face and his sword back in his hand. He side-stepped out from behind the table, and Shamhat matched him step for step. When he reached the edge and stepped forward, hate in his face, she stepped back, and grinned.

“Yes,” she purred. “Dance with me!”

When Himitsu hesitated, she called out the orders his *sensei* had given for sword practice, called him to his forms.

Step. Thrust. Step. Slash.

At each motion, she stepped just out of his reach, sometimes back and sometimes to the side.

“Tell me what she is to you,” Shamhat demanded. “You cannot know what she is to herself. Tell me, instead, why she matters enough to be brought back.”

“She is my safety.” Step. “She is my hiding place.” Thrust. Faster and faster, they danced, and Himitsu poured out his heart, his hurt, his hope, his shame.

“She is the last I have of my father!”

Shamhat stepped forward, within Himitsu’s reach, and slapped her palm flat against his heart. At the same moment, the new body meant for Moe jerked on the table, and then sat up.

Moe looked over and saw Himitsu and Shamhat, both covered in sweat and breathing heavily. She saw Himitsu with new eyes, eyes that had been sewn in by his mother, not placed by a factory worker.

"Listen to me!" Moe shouted.

Himitsu turned from Shamhat and hurried to Moe. He offered his hand, and she threw her arms around him, ignoring his sweatiness.

"But listen," she repeated. "The Library is dying. We have to save it."

"What happened to you?" Ivy asked.

"The Librarian struck me down," Moe said, "but there was a good reason for it. He didn't have enough spark on his own to bend the rules, so I loaned him mine. Victor was lying to us. Ask the Librarian about it so he can tell you."

Himitsu was suddenly angry again. "He did this to you? He's going to pay."

"Stop! Wait," Moe said. "Didn't you learn from what happened with Kenji? When I was gone, I could see it all. Listen before you get angry. I agreed to it, knowing you loved me enough to bring me back."

Shamhat, somehow no longer covered in sweat, placid as though she'd been watching tv this whole time, smiled languidly at them.

"I'm pleased you have your companion back. It's time for you to go now. Please conduct your business with the Librarian elsewhere. I have other appointments to keep."

She pulled a rope and in the distance, a bell rang. The Librarian opened the door and led them out of the room and back into their usual place in the Library.

Harmwala and Janice had observed the whole process with interest. If they were going to escape the Library walls, perhaps escape walls altogether, they'd need Ivy to tell their story. The way in which it needed to be told had surprised them.

It seemed a lot to ask, but only because they didn't know how much Ivy loved them.

Chapter Eighteen

Simon was having the best day of his life. He didn't know yet that it was the best day of his life, but it was. When we last heard about Simon, he was firmly ensconced in the land of Nod.

Simon might reasonably have expected, upon waking, to find himself alone if he had been a first-time visitor to the Library and not brought friends with him. This was not his first time. And he had brought friends.

This is why when Simon woke up, he found his friends waiting for him.

Elizabeth in her stamp and Mary on her stump were chatting with each other. Amiably might be too strong a word for it, but at least neither was trying to destroy the other.

"Simon," Elizabeth announced in her most imperious tone when she saw him awake, "Mary and I have decided that I shall be the ceremonial queen. And because I am in charge of ceremonies, let me welcome you back to the land of wakefulness." One might suspect that Elizabeth had decided to salvage what dignity and power she could, rather than fighting against clearly superior Powers. One would be right.

Elizabeth turned away from Mary and waved her arms above her head. She shouted out to a crowd outside of Simon's view. "He's awake, begin the march!"

Mary hopped up and down in excitement, each bounce making a pleasant springing sound that provided a beat for the marchers. Simon sat up and shelved the atlas—old habits being hard to break—and soon saw the new arrivals.

Dozens of chalk boys and dogs were headed his way. Some had black eyes, or only one arm, and some of their striped shirts were ripped. Most of the dogs had bandanas around their necks, and some had only three legs or legs of different lengths.

The biggest boy ran to Simon and reached out his arms to hug him. A little puff of chalk dust leapt from the wall, and then the others followed, and then Simon had his arms full of small boys and excited dogs leaving chalky prints all over his clothes.

"We've missed you, Simon!"

Simon was overwhelmed again. When he'd seen the fire, it had seemed that the world was coming to an end once more. Instead, he was being reunited with all of his old friends. All but one, at least.

If the matter of the Library's oncoming death were not pressing, I would relay to you all of the things that the boys, all named Jacob, and the dogs, also all named Jacob, had to say. We have time for a summary: "We've missed you Simon, and we're so happy to see you again."

When Simon had been abandoned by the Library, or perhaps when he had abandoned it—after so many years it was difficult to keep track of which was true—he had thought his friends lost.

On first entering the Library decades ago, he had taken his friend the boy Jacob with him. When Jacob had been unable to leave, Simon had drawn a dog to keep Jacob company. Each time he'd come back, Simon had drawn another boy and another dog, hoping that he could build an army large enough to break the spell that kept them trapped inside.

We know already that it was not a spell but a rule, and no amount of chalk could have let them escape the Library unless the rule changed or Simon was willing to expose his heart and let Shamhat make copies.

Now, his army of friends crawling on him, Simon let tears of joy flow from his eyes. One of the dog Jacobs tentatively licked at the stream with its tongue and then jumped back barking in surprise at the salt. With this army back, perhaps he could still destroy the Library and free them.

Elizabeth grew impatient. "Jacobs! Form up into your regiment," she commanded, and the boys and dogs slithered down to the floor and then up the wall to join the two girls. They formed around the edges of Elizabeth's stamp, each grabbing the edge with hand or paw.

"Madame Prime Minister," Elizabeth said, and Mary nodded to her, "take us to the letter."

Mary wobbled herself back and forth to get some energy stored up, and then bounded along the wall. Simon followed close behind her, and Elizabeth and her coterie of admiring Jacobs trailed after.

They traveled thus by commodius vicus past the re-circulation desk and to the stacks of recent additions. It didn't take Simon long to find the letter. He didn't have gloves, so he took off his socks and placed them over his hands.

I've been given permission to show you the letter. It's not like Simon is in a position to say no.

My Dearest Brother Simon,

I know you're unlikely to ever see this letter. Even if I decided to post it, I've lost track of your whereabouts. That's probably for the best.

Before I become maudlin at my condition, I'll say it plainly. I have liver cancer, and the doctors assure me with the best intentions that I'll die soon. I've made my peace with death, though not with what comes after. There are still people I owe, and you are one of them.

It was not right of me to blame you for our parents' deaths. When I was young I thought it was always obvious how to do the right thing. Only terrible people did terrible things.

I find myself hoping now that that's not true. I've done a terrible thing and realized too late what it was. The one I wronged has died. It looks like I'll follow close behind, and the speed with which my soul is dragged to Hell and punishment will, I hope, act as a counterweight to rush hers up to Heaven if she hasn't made it there yet.

I am too weary to write more, knowing that you'll never get this, but I can finally admit one thing. You know about your nephew Jirou, but you also have a niece. Her name is Ivy, and you would love her.

Farewell, brother.

Jacob

I was as surprised as you might be now. The filing notes say the author died the day before the Library was delivered to Ivy, and two days before the first attempt at delivery to Himitsu.

———

The revelation that Simon had a niece named Ivy, in all likelihood *our* Ivy, created a sense of urgency in Simon. He needed to get to this girl and tell her that though she was an orphan, she had family in the world who would love and cherish her and hope for the best for her. That was more important than his chalk friends.

He hoped, too, that she would return the favor. He

hoped that though he would still be an orphan maybe she could learn to tolerate him. Perhaps, one day, to like him. Some of his students had liked him, before he fell apart.

Simon knew he would never meet his nephew Jirou, so Ivy was all the family he could expect to have in the world. Just because Simon was wrong about Jirou—our good friend Himitsu—does not change the fact that he knew his nephew was lost to him. People often know things that aren't true.

Simon wandered the Library for a while looking for the others, hearing about the japes and jests of the chalk Jacobs while they walked. He knew from having spent a long time in the Library as a child that it would be as big or as small as it needed to be. A library so big that one couldn't reach the necessary books in a lifetime was as useless as a library that never contained the books at all.

After a while, he and his entourage heard yelling in the distance. One of the people yelling was the Librarian, which probably explains why he wasn't trying to hush the yellers. That, and the books already knew all the things that were being shouted out, so there was no need to keep it secret from them.

Simon followed the sound as it got louder and louder, and eventually came to the door that led out to the hallways and to Shamhat's room. The noise was coming from the other side, so he opened it.

"Am I coming out, or are you coming in?" he asked

those in the hallway.

"We're coming in," the Librarian said, as though that settled things. True to his word, he came in. The others, having no reason to remain in the hallway without him and a strong desire to continue their loud confabulation, followed him through the doorway, and Simon shut the door.

Without them much noticing, Simon herded them to a nearby seating area. This was a skill he had honed in his time teaching school. The students at his school had often liked to stand around arguing and enjoying each other at the end of the lunch line, which tended to create a backlog of hungry students wanting to pay but not being able to reach the cashier.

Even the Librarian sat.

Simon, because he had not been there at the start of the conversation, asked them to start again. With only a bit of cajoling, they agreed.

"The Library is dying," Moe said.

"And the Librarian always knew it," Ivy added.

The Librarian seemed to be feeling picked on, as much as a mechanical man can feel picked on. "I wasn't allowed to say so until someone asked me. There are rules to these things."

"How long has it been dying?" Simon asked.

The Librarian looked at Simon. He knew something was different—Simon seemed more alive than he had before—but he didn't yet know that Simon had found his brother's letter. "Since you first arrived. I had hoped you would help me save it, but you never asked the right questions. And then you left me."

"But I," Simon began. He had no excuse, and for the first time in a long time, he didn't try to invent one. "I did. I'm sorry." Simon noticed the Librarian didn't apologize.

Himitsu, our man of action, asked the question nobody had thought to ask before, and which the Librarian couldn't answer until someone asked. "How do we restore it?"

The Librarian held his hands out toward the others, but close to his body with the palms up, how one would prepare to catch a baby being thrown from a speeding car.

"We need more visitors. You may have noticed that the three of you humans are the only ones here."

"There's Shamhat," Ivy said.

"Shamhat is not human. Perhaps she used to be, in the original, but she is perpetually renewing herself by making copies. This doesn't work with ordinary copies, which each introduce new mistakes, but she has mastered the process. A gift from her first king. She is thousands of years old."

"What about the man upstairs?" Ivy asked. It wasn't that she was trying to be stubborn. She'd always been this way. She suspected that the Librarian was using the man upstairs as an excuse. Probably there was no man upstairs. She was wrong. And right. You'll see.

"The man upstairs is human, but, well, maybe it would be better to go and see. I am severely constrained in how much I can explain without you asking the right questions."

The Librarian stood and led them to another door. When they followed him through it, they found themselves in a large elevator. Simon pushed the up button. He'd been here once before, on the day he was punished for destroying the letter his father had written just before the fire to try and explain what was about to happen.

Simon still did not regret that destruction, but having been punished, he did not fear further consequence.

"It's not really upstairs if it's an elevator, is it?" Ivy smiled. She had been worried about the stairs, if she was honest with herself.

Simon nodded at her and resisted the urge to put his hand on her shoulder. He'd tell her soon what he'd discovered, but he didn't want to startle her quite yet. He could, however, share the secret that he knew.

"It's not a man, either," he said, and laughed. "But I have a feeling you'll love Emily."

Chapter Nineteen

Emily Dickinson waited impatiently for the group. She didn't mind being alone. Typically, she preferred it. But there was so much to accomplish and so little time to get it all done. She sat in a comfortable chair behind a large desk on which there sat a pedestal that she used to prepare flowers for pressing. Flowers were hard to come by these days.

At the end of things, she knew, this form that she now inhabited would cease to be. She would crawl back into her books of poetry and pressed flowers, her spirit to be let back out only when her words were read out by dreamers and destroyers.

Better that than greeting cards.

The humans and their companions arrived. The Librarian arrived last of all. Emily heard them come but sat looking up, out the window, the only one in the whole Library that looked onto the real world, until the last of the birds lifted from its perch and flew off.

"This will be less confusing if you save your questions until the end," Emily said. "But I know some of the questions that everyone always has, so I'll start by answering those."

"First, yes, these are sweatpants and a sweatshirt. It's so much more comfortable than what was available in my time. I would have worn it then if I could have."

"Second, I am that Emily Dickinson, but also I am not. The original me died a long time ago, and this is just the creative spark, which continues for as long as people remember you. I enjoy correspondence and don't mind being alone, so I have been a good fit for the Library."

"Third, the Library is indeed dying. Something in the basement archives is gnawing away at it. There was a time when I thought that it was mere apathy, that the Library was in decline because people did not care to read anymore. This is why the archives exist, after all, to accept the things nobody cares about anymore. Twenty-five years ago, which is recent for me, I noticed a precipitous drop in the number of visitors. Ordinarily, the Library should be full of patrons. Most of them will visit us in their dreams, read some things that may be true or mere fantasy, and return to their lives feeling more hopeful and ambitious."

"The dreamers stopped arriving. We could never admit many people through actual doors, and it has taken all of our resources to get the three of you here. Your imaginary friends should have come in through the dreaming doors. If they had, they would not be trapped now. Dreams are always fragments of reality and are not diminished by being copied. The same rules that were intended to keep things running smoothly are now being perverted to grind them into the dust."

Ivy processed everything that had been said and recovered more quickly than the others. "What do you need us to do?"

"I need you to go into the basement, find out what is stopping people from using the dreaming doors, and fix it."

Himitsu snorted. "Is that all?"

"No," Emily said. "You carry the ghosts of two fathers on your back. You'll need to resolve that before you can safely enter the basement. It won't guarantee your safety, but without doing that, I can see that you're doomed."

"You're a fortune teller now?"

Emily laughed. "Goodness, no. Just when you've been around for as long as I have, you learn to spot things. Off with you all, please, except for you, Ivy."

The others headed to the elevator, leaving Ivy alone with Emily.

"I can still see you," Emily called out to Harmwala, who had tried to hide herself along the wall behind a potted flower. Harmwala grumbled, but she, too, left.

Emily regarded Ivy seriously. So much would be riding on her shoulders. It should never have come to this, but not everything can be avoided.

"Listen to me. You must be the heart for the group. The boy and the man have their own strengths, but honesty with themselves is not one of them, and I am sure that will be the most important part of this fight. The imaginary friends are reflections of different parts of each of you. They are real, of course, but they are not independent of you."

"Why are you telling me this now?"

"You should have had a mentor earlier in the process, who could have explained these things to you."

"Why didn't I?"

Emily blushed. "We didn't have the budget. There's only so much we can do with the limited flow of dreaming that is reaching here."

Emily had stopped speaking, and Ivy sensed that she ought to go. She also sensed that despite being the man upstairs, despite being the one in charge, Emily wanted something that she wasn't able to ask for.

"Emily, did you want something else?"

"I want to give you a hug. Only if it's alright."

Ivy nodded, and Emily came around the desk and hugged Ivy tightly. "I'm sorry this is going to hurt so badly," she said.

Ivy had heard this often from doctors testing her limits. She'd heard it mockingly from kids who then pushed over her wheelchair and made her drag herself along the ground and struggle back into it. She'd heard it coldly from a world that didn't want to admit she was more capable than most in some things and less capable in others. Just like everyone else.

Ivy had heard this before, but this time she believed it.

Chapter Twenty

Moe quickly discovered some benefits to her new body. Most noticeably, she was much more flexible than she'd used to be. She was shorter now, so she had to walk faster to keep up. Still getting used to her legs, she'd tripped and fallen on her face. Instead of becoming stuck the way she'd used to, though, she simply pushed herself back up to her knees and stood up.

Oh, this was worth all of the losses! She would deal with not having a video camera to record or an Internet connection to look things up online. Having the ability to simply stand if she fell was amazing. By habit she reached her mind to check her battery level, and realized she had been freed from that tether, too.

Already the time that she'd spent dead was fading. Well, not dead. Deactivated? Incognito? Absent from the narrative of her life, anyway. She had said the most important thing on her return when she'd warned the others that the Library was dying.

For a moment, she'd had a clear vision of humanity

and its friends as a great web of connections. Some areas were snarled and some were sparse, and ideas stalked the webs as great spiders and the blue-uncertain-stumbling buzz of flies. Some of the flies had shed their bottleskins and emerged as spiders themselves, turned to devour their captors.

The important thing, thought Moe, was to be there for Himitsu's rebirth, just as he had been there for hers.

———

When Ivy found the others, they were already engrossed in going through a pile of letters. Ivy felt a twinge of concern that Himitsu might be touching them without gloves since she had her own gloves sitting on her lap, but then she saw that he was wearing a pair.

"You had extra gloves all along?" she asked the Librarian, hurt. She'd had to delay her own reading to go and buy gloves when he could have just given her some?

It was then that she noticed the Librarian's hands. Ivy had seen scars before, of course. On her friends' scabby soccer knees, their bicycle-fall elbows, the unearned and lied-about curling-iron burns on their backs. Ivy had seen scars before, and so she recognized the humanness of the Librarian's now gloveless hands, mottled scar and faded ink.

"It is important," he said, "that we not dawdle. We don't have time for illusions of otherness."

Ivy knew what it was like to be the object of stares, whether pity or disgust—which are not really all that different—and so she turned to the task.

Even though Simon was familiar with the Library, and Himitsu was looking for information about his own family, Ivy was the best qualified to help in the search. She had read the guides about how to use the Library, and she had the experience doing research on new topics for her cheating clients. Naturally, she took charge.

"We should start with your name, Himitsu. The main documents won't be stored there, but you should have a file that points to everywhere that you're mentioned. That will get us to your biological father's file."

"Hayashi Jirou," he reminded her. He'd told her before, during their long talk, but it seemed important that he voice it now.

Simon visibly paled, which was quite a feat for someone already so pale. "I know where the file is," he said, and went back to where he'd found his brother's letter.

He pulled out one of the older letters, the one in which his brother had told him the story of his doomed wife and their two children. Simon had burned this letter when he got it, but he couldn't be angry, now, that the Library had a copy. His fingers trembled, and he hesitated. Some of his chalk friends scurried across the floor and up his clothes and whispered courage in his ear. He handed the letter to Himitsu.

"You should read this," Simon said. "Your father is my brother." He turned to Ivy. "And my brother is your father," he told her.

Ivy knew this was a lie. Henry was her father. Ivy knew this was the truth. She was Jacob's daughter.

It's easy to forget we're part of the snarled web, not trapped by it.

———————

Simon,

I wish I was writing with happier news, but there's nobody I can think of who will better understand what's happened. Maybe you can explain it to me, as someone who knows? You're the only person I know who would do this kind of thing.

My wife and child are dead. Jirou survived, but I can't stand to look at him. I'm going to leave him with his grandparents. He's their problem now.

Mei went to the Yada river to take the boys swimming when I was at work, which she's done a lot of times before. It shouldn't have been a big deal, but she shouldn't have taken them so soon after a storm. Maybe she was lying, but she said that Jirou ran into the water to play with another boy and then Taro ran after him.

Mei said the boy was being too rough with Taro, and so she went to separate them. Somehow she pushed the boy hard enough that he was swept away by the current, and Taro, trying to get to him, was also pulled under.

Jirou was safe on the shore, but both the other

boys drowned, and then the police came to question Mei. It turns out she had been having an affair with the other boy's father, and he broke up with her. She confessed all of this to the police.

The police now think she drowned the boys as revenge. Do you think so? She denied it, but sometimes people lie about meaning to kill their family, don't they?

After her parents and I went to sleep, she went to the roof and leapt. Her mother says the ghost will haunt the apartment now, but her mother always was a moron.

I can't handle a kid alone. I don't even know the little thing. I'll write when I know where I've gone.

Brother and now widower of killers,
Jacob

Chapter Twenty-One

"He sounds absolutely awful," Ivy said. Certainly, the letter that they had just read presented an unpleasant side of Jacob. "But the death of your mother and brother, Jirou, is not his fault. I don't know if it's her fault. People can make mistakes and then get so wrapped up in guilt that they feel like there's no forgiveness. I think they're usually wrong. Sometimes there's no forgiveness from the people you've hurt, but if you change into a different person, the kind of person who would never have hurt them in the first place, you can learn to forgive yourself."

Ivy was not ordinarily given to long speeches, but she had taken what Emily said seriously. If Himitsu became despondent, or if Simon lost faith, then they risked the entire Library.

Because Ivy had so little left that tied her to her own life—despite her happiness, the web of humanity had gotten very sparse near Ivy since her parents died—she cared more about the Library than about the real world.

Particularly now, when without it she would be

without both her uncle Simon and her brother Jirou. The things that are real are those that are real to the heart. The Library was the most real place anywhere, for her. There would be time, later, for the anger at the lies her parents had told her. For sadness at so much lost time. Just as she'd kept moving forward when her parents had died, she'd keep moving now, knowing it would all catch up with her sometime. But not now.

Simon would take some adjusting, and perhaps a few showers, before Ivy would feel a deep kinship with him, but she had seen the way that the people in the park loved him. There must be some goodness in him. And some bravery to help them, when he could so obviously walk out and draw himself some more chalk friends. Why else would he be with them?

And Himitsu—Jirou, she reminded herself—was another thing altogether. She found him funny, if very angry, and liked being around him. Knowing now that she was his sister, she was really glad she hadn't kissed him. She didn't speak Japanese, and he didn't speak English, and so without the Library she had little way to communicate with him.

If the two children had known Jacob, though, before he became so bitter, and before he did so many horrible things and was hurt in such ways, they'd have realized that the unpleasant side of Jacob exposed by the letter was only one of many, many unpleasant sides to him.

For years, Simon had tormented himself with the belief that he could have done something differently to stop his father. And, eventually, his brother Jacob had realized that nothing could have been done differently. This was not much relief for Simon because it had come at the cost of two children and a woman.

Only when his own count of dead would have outweighed Simon's did his brother forgive him.

Only when Simon heard his surprise niece forgiving the man who had wronged her mother, who had taken from her the bond of having her father be her real father (I knew Henry well, and Simon was wrong about this part, but this was his thinking) could he admit that he deserved forgiveness from himself.

He was dizzy with the weight of guilt lifting off of him. Undoubtedly, it would stamp its foot back down on him from time to time, but he could see a future for himself. Perhaps he could get himself cleaned up and have his teaching license re-instated, after he finished things here. If burning down his life wouldn't work to get a fresh slate, there must be something else that would.

———

Ivy helped Himitsu follow the threads that extended out from his own documents to the things that had been written by and about his father. The real one, who had loved him and raised him until his early departure when Himitsu was only Ivy's age.

Even in death, he was not a talkative man. The section that should have contained all of his writings was empty. Himitsu saw things that his mother had written about him, but looking through these did not provide much insight. Himitsu would have given up if it were not for Ivy's insistence that there must be something to see. The man upstairs would not have encouraged him to seek out information about both of his fathers if there were nothing.

Finally, following the thinnest of threads, finding a document that did not mention Himitsu's father by name, only by implication, Ivy found something, a diary entry from the day that Himitsu's father had died.

"Today was another human body accident. They warned us when we learned to drive the trains that such a day would come, but I did not understand how terrible it would be. I had hoped it would never happen to me. It has made me doubt what I saw. The wife believes in ghosts, but I have always laughed at her for it. I should apologize because I don't know how else to explain it. I didn't see the man falling from the platform until it was too late. We're supposed to watch for people. I didn't know how much good it would do, but I always watched. Except today, because there was a woman in front of the train, so I had already applied the brakes. I would swear it on my grandfather's grave. And the man must have seen her too.

He was an old man, but he moved so fast, leaping down from the platform and pushing the woman out of the way just before I hit him. Everyone else swears there was no woman. But if there was no woman, what was he pushing? Why was he there?"

There was indeed a woman there, but she belongs in another story, and so her intrusion into Himitsu's story felt, to him, like betrayal. When her life was saved at the cost of another, she found her way back home and loved her children fiercely, if brokenly.

Himitsu flipped through the diary, trying to see if anything else was related. The other entries were obscured, unreadable because Himitsu did not have permission. The Library's encryption of private documents relies on the pattern of the human heart, not simple numbers, to keep what's secret away from those who don't need to know. Ivy assured Himitsu that the clarity of the entry meant it was certainly his father being talked about.

For years, Himitsu had cursed his father as a coward, who had run rather than staying to face whatever problems he'd had. He needed to tell Kenji that his father was brave, that his father had run toward danger to save someone else. Not just Kenji. He needed to tell his mother! He could, he believed, end her years of anger and shame. What he would reveal could let her get out into the world again and live a full life, instead of locking herself away in the apartment.

He explained all of this to Moe in his excitement, and Moe asked him to pick her up. In her old body, she hadn't liked him to hold her. The uniform was embarrassing, and he wasn't always careful about where he grabbed. This new body was soft, and made for hugging. Moe took full advantage and wrapped her arms around Himitsu's neck. "You should tell her. But doesn't this sound like what knowing has done for you?"

Himitsu wept, and Moe made room for Ivy's arms and for chalky boys and their dogs.

Harmwala and Janice felt left out, but this happens sometimes. It's hard to feel too sad for them. At least they weren't moldering on the mural wall, like poor Fred.

———

Moe felt some trepidation when she approached the door. Though she knew that, in theory, she ought to be able to leave the Library, having been forcibly rebuffed made her a bit nervous. Fortunately, she was not impeded in leaving, and Himitsu followed closed behind her.

They found Eri working. She had been enjoying the quiet with Himitsu and Moe finally out of the house during the early morning. Eri liked to sew while the sun shone through the windows and heated the room. In the spring, the aroma of the *kinmoku*, the fragrant olive tree whose flowers are prized for their scent, was blown in through the drafty windows and sweetened the apartment.

During the winter, she enjoyed the smells of food delivery cycles driving past with lunches for office workers. Contentment is cultivated, not obtained from circumstances. Eri had been growing hers for many years, and now Jirou was here to disturb it. She could tell from the look on his face.

"Welcome back, son."

Himitsu bobbed his head in greeting. "I have some news about father. He was a hero."

She smiled. "Yes, I know. Moe-chan, I am pleased to see you in the new body. It suits you well."

Being inside a body that Eri had sewn, loving with a heart that Eri's fingers had crafted, Moe knew the woman even better than she knew Himitsu. Even when there had been enmity between the two, it had been honest.

"Auntie, he means that when your husband passed on" (here, she's said *naku narimashita*, *become lost*, which is gentler than what can be said in English, but does not pretend it is something other than death) "he was not seeking to do so. Instead, he was trying to save the life of a woman who was on the tracks."

Eri smiled at Moe. "I know you are trying to be kind. Truly. I have never been upset with my husband for the manner of his death," she lied. People often lie when they hear what they most want. It lets them salve the wound, to say "oh well, I was lying too" if the news turns out false.

This part was true, though: "The train company had already informed me that because the circumstances were unusual, they would not be asking the usual payment for someone who has inconvenienced the train with their suicide. The truth is that he had left long before he finally died. His job had let him go because he had trouble keeping track of which day it was, and sometimes which year it was. We both pretended, for a long time, that he was heading off to work every day. You cannot abandon a person merely because they are inconvenient."

Himitsu felt inchoate shame at this, though he could not have named it. His mother was not thinking of him when she said it.

"I have been upset with him that he has not come to visit me since he died. My daughter has come sometimes. You must know, by now, what happened to her. But my husband has never come. I have hoped he found somewhere else to be. As much as I miss him, it is better to move on."

Himitsu knew, now, that the voices he had often heard at night, which he had thought belonged to his neighbors (the walls of their apartment being thin, and the neighbors being noisy), had belonged instead to his mothers. Why had her ghost never come to visit him? Himitsu did not know that she had used to visit him, when he was very young, but he had cried out in fear and she had gone away in sadness.

Later, when she might have tried again, his habit of leaving video games or Internet chat open while he slept had interfered with her ability to be seen. Ghosts are shy and fragile, and they require the edge of attention. Focus too keenly on them, and they are seen through, and vanish. Ignore them too stolidly, and they cannot surmount the liminal threshold. Sometimes when Himitsu practiced with his sword, when he was intently focused on breath and movement without thought, the ghost of his brother Taro sat, and watched. If only Ivy could restore me, I would tell him that. He had only been alone because he had shut his heart to all the people around him.

You see so much when you're in one of the in-between places.

———

Jirou and his mother talked for a long time, and Moe joined them, telling her Auntie how Jirou had revived her by being brave enough to share the contents of his heart. This is the only way any of us are ever saved, despite how it may look at times.

They talked for long enough that Ivy went home to get some sleep. The day's events so far had worn her out. Janice and Harmwala stood guard at the threshold to the house, though they couldn't yet leave the Library.

Simon slept on the Library floor. Ivy was his niece, but he didn't feel right, at least not yet, imposing on her. The Library was warm, but not too warm, and dark, but not too dark, and no men would come by to roust him or beat him for sullying their city. His many friends were with him, and it was enough.

Both Himitsu and Ivy prepared for what they had been told would be a final confrontation. For Himitsu, preparation was asking his mother, at Moe's urging, for as many of the empty doll bodies as he could carry in a backpack. For Ivy, her time was spent reading the poems of Emily Dickinson and writing letters to her parents. Perhaps there was a library where they were, and they could read how much she loved them and missed them.

Himitsu's mother had one final gift for him. She stood on a stool and reached up and far into the back of the closet in her room. She set a long box on the kitchen table and then opened it. Inside was a *guntou*, a Japanese military sword, with a leather scabbard. *Guntou* are functional swords meant to be carried by soldiers, who can be compelled to care for their weapons but will not love them the way a samurai would have.

"It was your great grandfather's," his mother said. "My father-in-law never used it, except in practice. I hope it will protect you more than it protected him, if necessary. I hope it will not be necessary."

Himitsu had never been a religious boy. His mother kept a shrine in the house, and when he was attending school he had sometimes said a little prayer to do well on an examination, but he was most observant around his sword practice. To be presented now with this ugly sword, which lacked any pretense about its purpose, was perhaps the closest he had come to what others might call a religious experience.

"I will protect it with my life," he promised. He bowed deeply to his mother and toward their shrine.

"Stupid boy," his mother said. "Protect your friends with your life if you must. But never an object. If this were one of the Three Imperial Treasures, it would still not be worth your life. Promise me: the only thing worth a life is a life."

Chastised, Himitsu promised.

Chapter Twenty-Two

Himitsu returned to the Library. Harmwala and Janice had been keeping watch over both Ivy and the door to Himitsu's apartment, and when Janice saw Himitsu return he called out to Ivy to let her know. She woke up and joined them after taking care of the necessaries.

After Ivy arrived, the Librarian led them to the top of the stairs down to the basement, where the problem seemed to have accumulated. Himitsu helped Ivy bump her chair down the stairs. They got all the way to the bottom before they noticed that Janice and Harmwala were unable to follow. The wall changed from wallpaper to unfinished stone of the sort you might imagine is in the walls of a castle, with a central column like a tree trunk holding up the ceiling. Indeed, the foundation of the Library had once been the foundation of a castle. And a pyramid. And a mud hut, and a church, and. Well, stories are part of every culture, and so the Library was built on many different traditions.

Nobody wanted to go on without Janice and Harmwala, so Himitsu helped Ivy back up the stairs, and the group went to visit Shamhat.

Well, most of the group went. Elizabeth and Mary, having made peace with one another, made their excuses, flimsy though they were, and declared they were going to visit Emily. Elizabeth had heard Emily was a lady, and Mary had heard she'd lived much of her life locked up in a tower. Simon agreed it was better they not come. They were already copies, and not very helpful ones.

In the room, Harmwala chose a body—tall, with skin the color of wet baobab bark and spots the color of ripe horned melon—from among those that Himitsu had brought. Ivy helped, but Harmwala did most of the telling of her own story, a story of nights talking with Grace, watching over Ivy, teasing her friends in the mural. Harmwala rose from the table in her new body and leapt down to try out this third dimension. Depth perception was trickier than she had realized, and it was surprisingly hard to be stealthy. Having feet made of soft fabric and bones made of stuffing was quite helpful, though, once she figured out how to not fall over. Harmwala's old shell, the now-faded paper resting on the wall, as though deeply asleep, seemed, to the new Harmwala, too small to have ever held her, even though it was much taller than this new body.

It was harder for Janice.

Himitsu had not brought any giraffe bodies. The necks of stuffed giraffes tend to break open when made to scale, and so they are not popular among people who purchase such things. Finally, he was persuaded to accept a body much like Harmwala's own with the pattern reversed, though the yellow was deeper and the spots were larger.

"My name is Chanda," he began, when it was time to tell his tale. Things went downhill from there. While Janice told his tale of bravery, of being the kind of male giraffe that his parents, should he ever meet them, would take pride in, Shamhat frowned at him.

"This will not work if you are lying," she scolded him.

This made Janice angry. "I am Chanda. I am a fearsome warrior, and I will not be spoken to in this way." He thought that if he got angry enough, maybe it would be true. In his heart, he knew these were lies. But also, in his heart, he didn't know what the truth was.

Ivy tried to help, but to no more effect than Janice's own efforts.

Harmwala sighed, enjoying the feeling when air puffed up her insides and was expelled. "I'll tell your story," she said. "I know you best of all."

And Harmwala danced for Janice. Her dance was the leap and scuffle of a predator but also the want-a-belly-rub vulnerability of a friend. "Janice is my best friend," Harmwala said. Ivy was surprised, but she supposed that it was alright. Fred, our deceased tiger friend, was Ivy's best friend, if only she had been willing to admit it.

Janice tried to join back in the dance, now that he

could feel his spirit being drawn to the new body. "I am Chanda!" he cried out. And his spirit moved a bit further from the body.

"Why do you keep insisting on being Chanda?" Harmwala asked him.

Janice lowered his head and licked his ears miserably. "Janice is a girl's name. If I were a girl, you wouldn't like me. Not in that way."

Most people don't know this, but hyenas, at least imaginary ones, can blush deeply enough to be seen through spots. Now, when Janice's story was being told, was not the time for lies or cowardice.

"Janice, I would like you, and yes, in that way, even if you were a girl. I've been a hyena and you've been a giraffe for years. It is not your bone bag that has made me love you. I love you. Do you hear with those ludicrous ears of yours? If you want to be a girl, be a girl. But your name is Janice, and so if you are a boy, Janice is a boy's name."

And Janice's spirit leapt into the new body as his heart embraced this truth. He pounced from the table down onto Harmwala, this boy with the boy-name of Janice, and showed her that his new arms were as good for hugging as they were for wrestling. He showed her how wonderful hands are for holding, and together they discovered some of the joys of having squishy bodies.

Let's give them a moment to collect themselves in private. They'll join us at the stairs.

Before long, Simon stood with his niece and nephew, with Moe and Janice and Harmwala, all now in the bodies Eri had made, at the bottom of the stairs, at the entrance to the underworld. His Jacobs roamed the floor in fits and starts, sometimes crawling up his legs to whisper jokes and secrets and warnings to him.

Some people, and I will not name names but you will probably know people of the type, suppose that art and history are less important than science. It is not a choice that needs to be made. A person such as Simon, such as you, can embrace them both. Humanity has told stories about the stars since humans first had eyes to view them and mouths to yell at them. It does not diminish the stars to know that they are impossibly distant and impossibly hot.

There are times they look cold and close.

As they wandered from room to room, Simon felt excitement building in him. He had trained as a historian, and the Library basement, its underworld, hinted at displays of ancient times that he had only dreamed of witnessing. As a child, he'd ventured down here, hoping to find his parents' letters without paying the Librarian's price, but he'd gotten lost and given up.

Despite Emily's assurance that the source of the obstruction to the dreaming doors was in the basement, there was nothing that seemed to be a candidate for the problem.

"Maybe we should try to find the dreaming

doors?" Ivy suggested when they had traveled for a while. Emily had told her that her heart would be needed, but beyond helping her friends, with one notable and stripy exception, to gain new bodies, she'd felt useless. She didn't see anything menacing.

Ivy closed her eyes and listened to see which way her heart suggested. One direction made her afraid, and so she suggested they go that way. Fear can be a warning of danger but also an indicator of pain.

Harmwala had spent many years stalking the jungle of the mural, despite it not being her natural habitat, and even in this new body she had the keen instincts of a tracker. She ranged ahead to see what was coming up. Being small and soft and (don't tell her I said this) adorable, she was at less risk of being noticed and harmed than, say, Himitsu, the muscular sword-bearer.

Janice followed nervously after Harmwala, not wanting any harm to come to her after he had finally risked and won by revealing his feelings after so many years.

Following the lodestone of Ivy's heart, the group made their way through room after room, impossibly many if the Library were not already impossible, until they found themselves shivering and confused, standing in a snowy parking lot, streetlight shining down and snow on the ground in front of them.

Ivy recognized the place and the car in front of her. This was the parking lot where she had performed her first task. This was the car that she had plugged in, though they had killed her parents. A woman was walking to the car with a young child. Ivy had tried so very hard to forget this woman, to banish her to the basement of her own mind.

The woman didn't seem to see Ivy and her friends, and Ivy knew that this was a movie for her benefit. She'd seen this kind of thing before, in the sillier sort of film. It felt quite different to be in it.

The woman put the child in the car, unplugged it, got in, and drove away.

Was this supposed to be some kind of test? Ivy was turning away in disappointment and confusion when a delivery truck began sliding, coming to rest with a loud crunch against the electrical pole where the car had been plugged in.

If the car had sat unplugged all day, the woman and her child would have been there trying to start it. The woman and her child would have been killed.

The way they deserved. Justice for killing my parents.

Ivy had seen how anger had tormented Himitsu, and she had hoped for him that he could outgrow it. Because she had paid attention to how it moved through him, she could recognize that this thought was not her own. It spoke in her mind, and it pretended to her voice, but these were not her feelings.

Standing outside of things, I could see what Ivy could not, though I could not warn her. Had she agreed with the voice, urged death on this woman for an accident, it would have given strength to the monster ahead and the monster inside.

Now that Ivy had recognized this, she warned the others. They followed Ivy's heart through the rooms, past Kenji being beaten by his father, Yugao having her heart broken when her friends betrayed her secrets. Past the smell of burnt hair in the bedroom where Simon's mother was caught, *in flagrante*, the night that she died on the day she had blackened Simon's eye.

These were the voices, unsilenced by denial, rage, or drink, demanding that hate replace dreams, vengeance replace hope, cynicism replace open-armed love. At each turn, Ivy grabbed a hand, sang a song, offered a hug. Whatever was needed.

Himitsu kept his sword sheathed.

Chapter Twenty-Three

Until its destruction in the thirteenth century, the House of Wisdom in Baghdad was the largest library in the world, appealing mostly to Islamic scholars. Simon had feelings about this, as we heard before.

The House's heyday was a few years before the invention of the Internet, and so although the House would have been an excellent source of photos to post for admiration, we have only a few illustrations left showing what it looked like.

Places have a spirit that transcends their mere architecture, and Simon recognized the House and warned his family.

"Are we moving back in time?" Himitsu asked this question.

Most people will tell you that time travel is, if not impossible, hugely impractical. This assumes that the travel happens in the way that an ordinary journey does, by walking or boarding a ship or stalking from tree to tree in search of bacon-on-the-hoof.

Most people deny time travel but know instinctively that it exists. All people travel forward, and most travel back. They pick up books or watch old movies or, if they're lucky, walk in the afternoon garden with grandparents.

Himitsu's question was a good one.

Our friends had been walking the wrong way through time since they entered the basement, first encountering Ivy's recent acts, and moving back from there. Death is this way, too, a reversal of birth, an undoing of the slow aggregation of atoms into bone, flesh, and song. The song quiets. The flesh decays. Finally, even the bone crumbles.

But I linger. The futility of my situation, that even now my paper is yellowing and becoming brittle and soon I will have nothing to make a copy from—it's bothering me.

In the House of Wisdom, Ivy and Himitsu explored, looking for the way forward, of course, but also enjoying time together as brother and sister. Thanks to the magic of the Library, they could read the ancient texts stored here, though many of them made little sense without context.

Simon explained different aspects of the collection to them, and Ivy saw that though Simon was still somewhat smelly and still wore socks on his hands to handle the documents, he was not the same man who had drunkenly threatened to burn down the Library.

"How long did it take you to memorize all this

information?" Ivy asked. She wanted to draw him out, to see more of the mind of this newfound uncle.

Simon laughed.

"I memorized some of it, but most of this I learned by reading and learning to understand how societies work and stop working. History is not about memorizing facts any more than mathematics is about memorizing numbers."

In the other parts of the library, patrons had been curiously absent. Here, they began to see more and more people, mostly men dressed in robes but also the occasional woman, walking through the building.

Moe tried to greet them, but they ignored her. She enlisted Harmwala and Janice, who were interesting to Moe now that they could interact on more equal footing, to help her in getting the attention of any of the people.

When that failed, Janice climbed up Ivy, hugged her neck, and asked for help. The humans had no better luck than their imaginary friends in attracting attention.

Are these the dreamers? Himitsu wondered. *Is this what it is like to be a ghost, trying to talk with anyone and being ignored?* I have some experience in this. Yes, that's what it's like to be a ghost. But these were not dreamers. They were echoes of dreamers past, when the House of Wisdom had been the Library, before it had been relegated to the archives.

Even the largest library in the world does not take that much time to walk through, and eventually the companions had explored the entire House of Wisdom, coming to a final plaza, which had packed sand on the ground and a pair of colossal stone legs sticking up out of the center.

With nothing else to do, they went to look at the legs. In front was a plaque:

My name is Ozymandias, king of kings: Look on my works ye Mighty and despair.

"Oh poop," Simon said. More or less. "That doesn't belong here. Shelley won't write that for another six centuries, and there's no evidence that Ozymandias ever made it to Iraq."

Moe perked up at the mention of Shelley, and there was a short digression while Simon told her that Percy Shelley was the husband of Mary Shelley, Victor's creator, and thus, in a sense, part of the pantheon of gods for Moe. Moe understood, after her visit to the web, that some Powers in the Library were working against progress.

"Ozymandias was what the Greeks called Ramses II, one of the pharaohs of Egypt. This doesn't belong here. Something is wrong."

Harmwala patted Himitsu's leg urgently to get his attention.

"Do you smell smoke?" she asked.

They did.

Soon, not only did they smell smoke but they saw

fire in the distance and men running at them with swords. Himitsu remembered what he had promised his mother. He did not draw his sword. He made sure his friends were with him, and he fled.

Moe, Harmwala, and Janice rode with Ivy, and the three humans hurried back through the House toward the edge of the city. Simon had trouble keeping up with Ivy and Himitsu, but the screaming warriors behind him provided incentive.

Finally, they came to a stop, panting and sweating, outside the House of Wisdom and watched it burn. The warriors had given up their chase at the edge of the House.

"Who were they?" Himitsu demanded of Simon.

"Those were the Mongols. This is bad. The destruction of the library is playing itself out again."

Even though Simon himself had called for this, he had done so in the abstract. Like many people, his words had expressed a willingness to violence that his spirit could not tolerate. The problem with this is that it encourages those whose spirits crave blood. It makes their own violent words seem like mere exuberance, rather than declarations of depravity.

Simon now regretted The Rant. Even after it had resulted in him being fired and ending up homeless, he had believed in it. His own tragic fire had convinced him that those who objected were craven weaklings, unwilling to face the chaos that can release growth. Most violence is in the service of order. It offers a going back, not a starting over. And most violence is quiet, measured out one mocking word at a time. Now, exhausted, lost, and near despair, he saw how brave it is to stand in the face of violence and reject it.

Soon, the artificial sun set, and the light of Baghdad burning was not enough to keep the humans and their friends from falling into fitful but dreamless slumber.

Ivy was the first to wake. Janice and Harmwala were awake soon after. They had always used Ivy as an alarm clock, sleeping when she slept and waking when she woke.

Waking up was a surprise to Moe. In her electronic body, the difference between sleep and wakefulness was a matter of battery discharge rate, of setting different levels of sensitivity for her cameras and microphones. This new body had none of those things. She was simply back, as though she had merely paused for a thought after the fire and then found the sun had moved itself. The change was disorienting, and she understood better now why Himitsu was always so grumpy in the mornings.

This disorientation was not entirely the fault of Moe's body. Ivy, too, was disoriented. Baghdad had disappeared. It was not burnt to ash, at least not that Ivy could see. It was simply gone, and where it should have been stretched a great river. We move through the past in fits and starts, forgetting some moments and remembering others until we convince ourselves that what we remember is all there was.

"Uncle Simon?" Ivy liked how it felt when she called to him. She'd never had an uncle before. "Can you tell me where we are?"

Simon sat up and rubbed his eyes. He had a wicked headache, and he really could have enjoyed a drink, but he was able to think clearly, and he had not overlooked what Ivy had called him. It made him smile.

"We're at a river," he said.

Ivy was beginning to learn that this was Simon's idea of a joke. She didn't think it was funny, but she suspected she had only to wait a moment and Simon would continue.

"This seems to be the Nile delta."

Ivy was impressed. "How do you know?"

"Because he," Simon said, and pointed to a man striding purposefully toward them over the sand, "is Julius Caesar, and if you look over that way" (he pointed) "you'll see both his fleet and the Egyptian fleet. This is the siege of Alexandria."

Knowing that this was not real, at least not in the way that people typically mean real, Simon was having enough fun that he mostly gave up on the idea of burning the Library. It would only entrench things more deeply, not allow starting over. He had studied these events and these people, but he had done so with the knowledge that the events were long past and the people long dead. And, let us remind ourselves, because of the magic of the Library, it was not necessary to know one of the many languages of the time to speak with the people. This aspect was the best for Simon.

Moe discreetly woke Himitsu, who had slept more poorly than either Ivy or Simon. Ivy did not usually sleep in her chair, but she could do so in a pinch. Simon typically did sleep on the ground, so the night had been little different from ordinary for him. Himitsu alone among them was used to stability and comfort in his sleep.

A cautious man would have hesitated to approach Ivy, Simon, Himitsu, and their imaginary friends. They were strangely dressed, and Himitsu was armed with a sword. The details have varied through time, but swords have been recognizable for thousands of years.

Julius was not a cautious man. Deaf in one ear and known to have seizures, he had nevertheless conquered much of his world and would soon force Rome to acknowledge him as its ruler.

"You there!" Julius called out, and pointed with his sword at Ivy. "What are you doing here? Who do you serve?"

"Oh heck no, I don't have to put up with that sand," Ivy yelled back. More or less. "I am nobody's servant!"

"Apologies, milady, I should have recognized you were a Nubian queen sitting on her throne, and not merely one of her servants."

Simon could tell that this had made Ivy even more

angry. He didn't know the history of this, not having grown up as Ivy had and looked as she did. "I don't think he means anything bad," he told Ivy.

"They never do," she spit back.

"Let me clarify," he told Ivy. "Parley?" he yelled back to Julius.

Julius agreed, and approached alone, even with Ivy glaring daggers at him. Julius would have a different relationship with daggers a few years in the future.

When Julius stood before them, clad in light armor and with his sword, even uglier than Himitsu's, in his hand, he knelt and saluted Ivy. Then, because Simon was the one who had offered parley, Julius turned to Simon.

"I seem to have given offense. Is she not one of the Candaces? She is in the wrong place and the wrong dress to be Egyptian."

Simon laughed, as deeply as he could remember ever doing so. He then apologized to Julius. Angering him was historically not a great idea, as the Senate would discover soon. "Let me explain to my lady," he said. "She is not entirely used to your language."

Ivy and Simon withdrew to talk privately while Julius and Himitsu talked about swords and battles, or whatever.

"So," Simon said. Ivy had gotten so mad he wasn't sure how to begin, and "so" is always a good starting point. "Julius thinks you are a Nubian queen."

"I heard that sand the first time."

"No, I mean, one of the queens of Nubia, which is not far south of here. At the moment, Nubia and the Roman empire are rivals, and Nubia is ruled by a queen. The queens are called Candace by the Romans. It's how the Romans say the Kushite word for queen. They are greatly respected as skilled rulers and military leaders."

"So he's not making fun of me? At school, they call me the Nubian princess, and laugh at me for how I talk."

Simon had been a teacher of kids Ivy's age. He'd thought he knew all the ways that children tormented each other, but growing up without parents to initiate him in the ways of scorn, he'd never heard the dog whistles that the children learned and then turned on anyone who didn't exactly fit.

"I promise you he's not making fun of you. You know who his girlfriend is?"

"Julius Caesar has a girlfriend? Who is it?"

"Cleopatra, Queen of the Nile. He's not thinking anything about your skin."

"Shut up!" Ivy was laughing now, and she wiped away tears she hadn't felt starting. How different would her life have been had she had teachers like Simon? Her parents had done everything they could, but when the world you see doesn't match what your parents say, it can be more confusing than inspiring.

"It's true! You should ask him. And you should ask him if we can go to the city."

And so Ivy's travel throne, as Julius insisted on calling it, and Simon's knowledge of history let our friends have a pleasant breakfast with the de facto leader of much of the world and then pass through the siege of Alexandria and into the city.

Chapter Twenty-Four

Himitsu had always imagined that places outside of Japan had, in ancient times, been awful slums in which suffering was the only choice. Alexandria challenged this notion. It looked very much like some of the older neighborhoods in Nagoya, differing only in the shapes of the houses and the color schemes chosen.

They passed several open storefronts with people using straws to drink beer from bowls and enjoying food prepared for them. Julius had assumed that Ivy was a queen, but the city residents seemed to know better. Her wheelchair attracted a few curious glances—chariots were known, so the wheel-and-axle system was not a surprise, but its application to such a small seat was—but she was otherwise ignored.

Himitsu, in contrast, was a person of great interest. The fineness of the fabric he wore (that is, the simple machine-woven cotton of his t-shirt) marked him as a man of means, and the excellence of his sword as a military man. It was the habit of some of the commanders to walk incognito among the men to assess their morale during this siege, but Himitsu did not look Greek or Egyptian.

The attention made Himitsu nervous. He was not one of those Japanese people rude enough to stare at foreigners in Japan. He checked to see where they were heading, and to see what language they were speaking, of course, but this was not the same at all. In other circumstances, Ivy might have taken pity on him. It was his first time being in a place where people did not mostly look like him. Ivy had experienced the reverse shock when she had gone with her parents to the Bahamas and people mostly did look like her.

These various things reminded them that they were not in Alexandria to sightsee. The city was not really around them, which was obvious from everyone speaking English or Japanese, depending on who we ask. Simon inquired at the nearest food stall, and the vendor pointed them in the direction of the library.

It was only a few tens of minutes away, and the well-tended roads of the city made the journey pleasant. Ivy was in love with it all. *When this is over, I'm going to ask Uncle Simon how much of this is real and how much is the Library smoothing our way.*

Because it was clear that the Library was assisting their journey as much as possible, the way all libraries smooth learning. Sand did not trouble Ivy's wheels the way that it should, Simon was not craving drink to the expected degree, and Himitsu did not find himself sweating and wishing for the dark and safety of his room.

The Library—the one upstairs—was not alone in its manipulations. They arrived at the local library and entered to find that the entry hall was filled with a set of cubicles. A person sat inside each cubicle writing on paper (and the use of paper was also wrong, as the papyrus scrolls organized elsewhere showed) and then burning the writing.

Ivy went and snatched a piece of paper from one of them and examined it.

"Millionaires want to ban this video!"

Moe brought her another:

"You'll never believe this one weird cure for illiteracy!"

And Janice brought another:

"Science proves atheists are evil and people from the south are dumb!"

Ivy was both confused and angry. "What are you doing? Why are you burning these?"

"They're sending them to dream lands," Himitsu said. "Offering them up as prayers." His mother sometimes did this, though he'd never asked her what she wrote. She'd come home, upset and smelling of incense, and it hadn't seemed to him his place to intrude.

"But what purpose does that serve? We're already in some other place."

"Maybe that's why the dreaming doors are clogged? These people are sending nonsense and hate as though it's dreams. With the Library recording everything that's written, wouldn't this overwhelm it?"

The workers had been ignoring them, but now Harmwala, who had been keeping watch, alerted the group to a new arrival.

Striding toward them, with the same smug confidence that the Librarian had exhibited, was a mummy. His face was bandaged, but the bandages lay tight against him and did not obscure his features. The pure white cloth trailed down his neck and disappeared into the collar of an equally white shirt.

The mummy was wearing a business suit.

"That's the idea," he said.

He held out a gloved hand, but nobody wanted to shake with him. He shrugged.

"I'm Ozymandias. We should talk. I think someone has been lying to you. Is Emily Dickinson still the man upstairs? She's had it out for me the entirety of her brief visit."

He gestured to an opening on the east side of the room. "Please, come into my office."

"This is bad," Simon said. "He shouldn't be here."

"Neither should you," Ozymandias retorted. "At least I'm Egyptian."

———

Ivy's mother had always done her hair for her. Ivy could do it herself, but it was one of the many ways that she and her mother spent time together. Sometimes, if Grace was particularly busy, her father might run a pick through it for her, but it had never been something that he felt confident about, and it wasn't the same. When Grace and Henry died, Ivy no longer had anyone to do her hair. Harmwala, in particular, was happy to offer advice, but for obvious reasons could not be much actual help.

Ivy had shaved her head. At the time that she'd done it, it had made sense to her. She told herself that it took up a large part of her day as she fussed over it, trying to get it just how her mother had done it. She didn't particularly care how it looked. Other people had always been much more invested in it than she had. In truth, it reminded her each day that her mother would never do it again. She had enough reminders of loss.

Maybe other girls could have gotten away with being bald. Certainly, the boys could do it and nobody would give it the side eye. But, though she mostly didn't notice it, Ivy was not like other girls, and the result was predictable to everyone but her.

People started either treating her as though she were invisible or coming to offer their so-sorrys and you're-so-braves when she was at the mall or even at the library. At first, Ivy thought perhaps they interpreted her shaved head as a sign of mourning. And she was in mourning, but how did they know?

Young children are often the best at dispelling our illusions, and that's what happened in this case, too. Ivy was at the library, per usual, and being a little bored (and, honestly, a little sad), she was zooming through the stacks. Quietly.

There was a rule against running, but she wasn't breaking that rule, and the librarian knew of her recent loss. The librarian assumed that Ivy was now living with relatives. All of the adults in her life assumed something like this: that she was living with relatives, or in a foster home, or that she had been adopted.

She had slipped through the cracks because everyone assumed someone else was taking care of her. Adults know that if you ask other people about their troubles, they might expect you to help them.

But a young boy at the library was jealous that Ivy got to run. To him, there was no difference between his own running and Ivy's rapid circuit around the library, except that his wasn't allowed.

"How come she gets to run, mom? I want to run."

"Hush. It's rude. And stop pointing. Look at her. Poor thing has got cancer. There's no need to take away the one thing that might make her happy."

It hadn't even occurred to Ivy that people would assume this. That wasn't what she wanted at all, and so she grew her hair back out, keeping it styled in the loose afro that was its natural state.

Because of this experience, Ivy tried not to make assumptions about people's medical conditions on the basis of appearance.

Still, it was natural to think that Ozymandias might not be in his prime, with all visible parts of him covered in bandages. He sat on a comfortable chair behind a comfortable desk, but without being able to see whether he was smiling, frowning, or grimacing (lack of a mouth makes it difficult to tell), Ivy wasn't sure at all how he was feeling.

"Mr. Ozymandias, are you in pain?"

Moe smiled at Ivy. The more time she spent around the girl, the more she liked her, and she was glad they were going to remain in each other's lives. She had sometimes worried that Yugao would take Himitsu away from her, but Ivy did not pose the same sort of threat.

"I am quite well, but thank you for asking. The bandages keep things tidy. Otherwise, bits are always sloughing off everywhere."

"And the suit?" Simon asked. He had always been distrustful of people wearing suits. People in suits at the park typically meant someone was going to try and kick them out. Before that, people in suits at the school had meant someone's budget was getting cut, and he could be sure it wouldn't be the computer lab's.

"I'm trying to bring a bit of dignity to the office. Ms. Dickinson has left us only the bits that are falling apart."

"Why are you blocking the dreaming doors?" Ivy asked.

Ozymandias explained, in tedious detail, the conservation of mass necessary for the Library to store so much, and how old things must constantly decay to make way for the new, and the underworld was where things were sent to be disposed of and blah blah blah. In short, Ozymandias disagreed with Emily's choices, being unhappy both that he was no longer in charge and that they had let a woman take the helm. He didn't look at Ivy while he explained, knowing that Himitsu and Simon were more likely to see reason.

Janice and Harmwala had more interesting ideas. While the big people were distracted, they wandered the office, peeking in drawers, looking out windows, and generally acting like curious but stupid cubs.

Maybe that's just my jealousy speaking.

In their exploration, they found that Ozymandias had a drawer full of what looked like candies. Some forms have their own magic, and if you have a set of cubicles outside a private office, candies will appear somewhere.

After checking that Ozymandias wasn't watching, they each took a piece. In a moment of terrible sweetness, Janice put one in Harmwala's mouth, and Harmwala returned the favor.

Their bodies didn't need to eat, strictly speaking, but they could do so. Going to all the trouble of animating a body hardly seems worth it if sensory experiences aren't included.

Janice began chewing, and each time that his mouth closed, someone screamed.

Janice stopped chewing.

Harmwala began chewing, and each time that her mouth closed, someone begged for mercy.

Harmwala stopped chewing, too.

They both carefully took the candy out of their mouths and threw it away.

But then the screaming started again. The begging started again. The candy hadn't caused the noises at all, but it would still be a while before the two would be eager to try unknown candies.

Simon was the first to recognize the characteristic noises of fire engulfing a building. "The building is burning!" He was nearly panicked, and Ivy reached out and held his hand to soothe him.

"Find us a way out, Himitsu," she said. She called those small enough to ride with her and loaded them up. If everyone had a job, then orderly evacuation was the most sensible course of action.

Ozymandias chuckled. "Of course the building is burning. That's why we're here and what I've been saying. We've got to get rid of the useless bits somehow. Everything burns on a schedule to maintain order. Think of it like a scary amusement park ride. People wouldn't accept actual chaos, but they're happy to pretend. Not to worry, though, there's a passage out."

He got up from his desk and walked over to a too-modern keypad, punched in a security code, and walked through the door that opened.

Having no better options, the others followed.

Chapter Twenty-Five

Growing up in Fairbanks, Ivy had seen the Northern Lights many times. It had ceased to be surprising after the tenth or hundredth time she had sat outside with Henry in the back yard on a cold evening while Grace made cocoa inside. Harmwala and Janice, likewise, had become plussed about the lights.

Context is everything. Seeing the Northern Lights here astonished everyone but Ozymandias. A moment ago, they had been in full daylight in the Library of Alexandria as it burned down around them. (Julius asked me to relay his apologies. He hadn't meant to set the library on fire, and he felt bad enough about it that he would go and steal another library to replace it.)

"Where are we?" Ivy asked.

"This is the usual entrance," Ozymandias said, "what you've been calling the dreaming doors. Please, everyone have a seat. This is a more pleasant backdrop for our discussion than the other office. The constant remodeling there can grate after a while."

Himitsu had been hoping for a fight since they'd first stepped into the underworld. In some versions of the Japanese underworld, samurai warriors challenge the traveler, and worth is displayed by fighting these samurai and, ideally, reciting poetry while doing so. Ozymandias was too urbane to evoke violence in Himitsu.

Ozymandias pointed them to movie theater-style seating, and they sat. Ivy sat at one of the ends next to Himitsu, and they held hands. When Yugao had kissed Himitsu, Ivy had been wondering whether she ought to develop some unsisterly feelings for him, but this sibling-feeling was much more comfortable for her. There had been boys before and there would be boys later. (I don't have the heart to correct her.) There was only this one brother, and so she did not regret the loss.

For a while, everyone sat and watched the lights. Ribbons of green undulated slowly across the sky, obscuring the stars behind them. Occasional streaks of purple flared brightly and then guttered out.

The floor was made of discarded notes, parking validation slips, receipts from shopping malls. Verbal debris, all polished until it was so smooth it reflected the light that descended onto it from above.

Had they all been patient people, they might have sat like that until the world stopped. It's often said that patience is a virtue, but like other virtues there is a point at which it becomes harmful. Fortunately, Himitsu was not a patient person.

He started fidgeting, and his hand was sweating where Ivy's touched it, and he wanted Moe sitting closer to him and Simon was still emitting something of an odor and, finally, his discomfort broke the spell.

He took his hand back from Ivy and clapped loudly. The percussive effects of that were far sharper than the soft hum being emitted by the lights and echoed by Janice. The others woke up, but found themselves overwhelmed by lassitude and unable to move.

Ozymandias sighed. "Ah well, it was nice while it lasted. Listen, isn't this beautiful? Each quantum of light is a dream of words denied entry here. In the old days, when I ran things, there weren't as many people wanting to come here. It was easy to get rid of everything that had been forgotten by the world. Look at you humans now, though! Billions of you, and so many of you read, and so many of you write. It's not sustainable. Reading used to be a privilege, something only a few people got to do, because they deserved it. Now you give it out like a medal for participation. 'Congratulations, human, on being born. Let's teach you how to read.' It's ridiculous. If everyone can read, how will the scribes make money? How will the powerful stay in power? Most importantly, how will I ever get all this work done with that woman running it? She's forcing me to burn the libraries, and she doesn't care. She's one of the worst offenders about making more work! Even when she was dead, she didn't stop putting new poems into the world. Maybe when everything stops, they'll finally see it was a mistake to put her in charge."

Moe finally found the energy to move by drawing on her schoolgirl programming, which was intended to make her the perfect student. She raised her hand and asked one of the set of questions intended to show her seriousness: "*Sensei*, should we be writing this down? Will it be on the test?"

As a former teacher, Simon knew when he heard the question that the script writer had a wicked sense of humor, and his laughter brought him entirely out of the spell.

Moe shook Harmwala until she woke, and then the two of them freed Janice. Simon and Himitsu brought Ivy around.

Ivy glared at Ozymandias. "Everyone deserves to read," she shouted, "and if you need more help then just ask for it. There's no shame in asking for help! When were you in charge? Thousands of years ago? Things have changed."

Perhaps if there had not been an audience, this appeal, and lots of discussion, could have shifted Ozymandias toward a different way of thinking. Perhaps. There is only so much magic in the world, and some people are not amenable to evidence. But now the trolls had arrived, summoned by Ozymandias being criticized. There were so many of them! Some of them were dressed in business suits and others in their pajamas. They were of all colors and sizes, and many of them were barely older than children. Ozymandias could not tolerate being embarrassed in front of anyone else. It was, in fact, this more than any dermal difficulties that led to him covering himself in bandages, dressing in the trappings of secular power, and blaming his failings on other people.

Ozymandias fled, content to let his underlings take care of the group. He hadn't asked them to do so. They were doing it on their own. Later, he could disavow their actions and keep himself, his suit, and his bandages clean.

Himitsu finally drew his sword. These trolls had the look of dreamers, not people who were really here in the Library, and so he did not have any qualms about destroying them. In response, the trolls brandished keyboards and video cameras pointed at themselves, typing and shouting foul imprecations intended to demoralize and finally overwhelm our friends. Some of them kept shouting at Ivy that she was pretty and should just smile. Show a little skin. Don't be such a tease. When she didn't humor them, they became angry and started calling her unrepeatable names.

Himitsu laid about him mightily with his sword.

One, two! One, two! And through and through the ugly blade went snicker-snack! Each troll exploded when it was struck, bursting into a cloud of angry words. A few of the trolls gathered their courage and charged, pens in hand, convinced by the others who told them the pen was mightier than the sword.

They were wrong. People who reject the value of art and literature often overlook metaphor.

Not to be outdone, Simon grabbed some of the trolls by the ear and read them the riot act. He was not, he told himself, defending the Library, only his family. Ivy laid about her with ferocious punches at the trolls who stooped down to mock her or demand a date or both.

It took less than half an hour to destroy all the trolls. Their power came from hiding their identity and attacking only the weak, retreating when they encountered resistance. Having been lured into exposing themselves here, they were easily defeated.

They had served their purpose, though. As in real life, they had provided enough cover for the one in charge to escape and had made life more difficult for those who dared to dream. Ozymandias was nowhere in sight.

———————

Himitsu had never struck anyone with a metal sword before. His practice sword was made of split bamboo and intentionally flexible. It hurt to be hit with a practice sword, but bruises were the worst that could be expected so long as the sword didn't break.

He felt powerful, seeing how his real sword had ripped apart the trolls. Without Ivy and Moe there to remind him of his humanity, he would still have chased after Ozymandias, but he might have been swayed to join his cause when they met.

When you're hurting, it can be a powerful salve to hurt other people. People are taught to deny this, but tigers are allowed to lust for the hunt, and to learn how to overcome this hunger. Some never learn this second part, and the villagers mourn even as they hunt down the man-eaters.

Moe climbed Himitsu. It was harder than climbing Ivy, whose chair provided convenient handholds, but Moe was glorying in the freedom that this body, built for the rough-and-tumble fun of children and pets, provided her. It was so much more fun than the collectible body she'd worn before.

"We're here to open the doors, not win fights," she reminded him.

He nodded. Angry as he was, excited as he was by the anger, he nevertheless calmed himself down. He drew on his training and on his experience with meditation to return to a calm place. But he did not sheathe his sword.

"We have to go after him," Simon said. "We don't know how any of this works, and anything we fix he'll just break again." Simon was more subtle, so everyone missed that these words were strongly rooted in fear, not thought. Sometimes, even smart people are wrong. I warn you now that there are hard times ahead.

Philosophers sometimes concoct problems in which there are only two choices, but these are intended as thought experiments, not reality. The trolley problem is a famous example. Suppose you're driving a trolley and you must make a choice between allowing the trolley to continue on its path, in which case it will surely kill five people, or changing the path of the trolley, in which case it will surely kill one.

Ordinarily, the question is whether to switch the trolley to the other path.

I warn you now, because I could not warn them: Simon's suggestion and Himitsu's anger, his choice to not sheathe the sword, are not the choice of whether to switch paths.

Their actions are the choice to unblock the wheels of the trolley, release the brakes, and start it on its murderous way.

———

They followed Ivy's heart, despite its misgivings, and hurried after Ozymandias through ice and desert, through empty stadium and weekend offices, everything sculpted of discarded words and without even the slow life of warring trees.

When Harmwala spotted faint tracks, their pursuit became even faster, and soon after the tracks became footprints and then deep furrows in the ground: deeper, larger, and closer together as they progressed.

And then Ozymandias was in front of them, at the stairway out of the basement.

Gone were the bandages.

Gone was the suit.

It was obvious now why the tracks had changed. Ozymandias had grown as he ran, taking on stone and word. His legs were almost entirely stone, and his skin, where it was not stone, was the color of wet newspaper. Every headline warned of doom.

"Friends," he said, and spread his arms wide. "I've taken pre-emptive steps to protect myself, as you can see. Perhaps we should call this a day? You go report to Emily that she'll have to content herself with a few visitors a year, and I'll go back to my task of helping people forget the past. When we know which man is heading upstairs next, we can revisit the issue."

"We can't let you do that," Himitsu shouted. "You're out of control, and you must be destroyed."

And though Moe shouted warning, Himitsu could not hear it. He wanted the past back, and here was the man who had destroyed it. He wanted time to go and listen for the ghost of his mother's daughter, to talk more with his father, to follow where his father's mind wandered.

He circled Ozymandias recklessly, his confidence bolstered by how easily they had beaten back the trolls. Simon tried to call Himitsu back from his anger. The Jacobs ran up Himitsu and whispered in his ear, told him that sometimes the way to move forward is to forget and forgive, but he swatted at them and continued his private war.

Himitsu lunged forward and struck, and the sword

became lodged in Ozymandias' arm. Like an unworthy supplicant before Excalibur, Himitsu could not pull it out. He tried, failed, fell.

And then Ozymandias took the hilt in his other hand, and pulled it free. "I'll regret this," he said, "but it won't be long before I forget."

Ozymandias, armed now with Himitsu's sword, shambled inexorably forward. The stone that covered his legs and was in the process of engulfing even more of him slowed his progress, but the three humans were trapped. He was powerful enough, grown strong on the concentrated repetition of hate, lies, and ephemeral gossip, that he could strike down all three of them without risk to himself. Even Ivy, who'd never trained with a sword, who'd never been woken by a kick to the ribs in the middle of the night, could tell they had lost. Having failed to beat Ozymandias and, worse, having armed him against them, no hope was left to them.

Simon, who was once more having the best day of his life, though it did not seem like it, did not find hope. Hope had abandoned him many years ago. But he found courage.

He alone could have run, back to the illusion of solitude, back to pretending the drink made him forget. Instead, he stood in front of the two children, and bellowed his defiance.

"Stop, dad! Don't burn us!"

Simon knew that Ozymandias was not his father.

He said it because he could not let himself die without having said those words at least once, even if they were useless. He had entered with the intent of bringing the system to an end so that he could start over, but love has a way of changing our plans.

Ozymandias struck, pushing the sword straight into Simon's heart.

Simon's heart stopped beating.

But Simon's heart had been stone for many years. I told you this before.

The stone of Simon's heart was pierced, and broke the sword.

The stone of Simon's heart was pierced, and the chaos that had been flowing through him burst forth in a cloud of chalk. Ozymandias was blinded by it, and as he tried to clear his eyes he found himself being carried away, one bit at a time, by chalk drawings of boys and dogs. There were two different kinds of boys, the Jacobs of before and the Simons of now, and they were smiling at each other. Laughing silently as they tore Ozymandias apart. It was the best day of their lives.

Children can be cruel sometimes. They may poke each other, call names, and pull tails. But children know how to forget their hurts, how to believe the true-but-impossible. Most importantly, no adult has the tolerance for repetition that a child has. It was this that was tearing Ozymandias apart. Ozymandias was going to be defeated.

Because the boys were chalk, he could not catch them except by gouging himself, which only created more dust to turn into boys and dogs. Because the boys laughed, delight rather than scorn, and were not afraid, the lie that formed his bones was stripped of its power. Because the boys, like children everywhere, asked the hard question—why why why why why—eventually Ozymandias ran out of places to hide, and his secret was exposed.

He was afraid. He had always been afraid. Fear is the father of hate, and hate is never a patricide.

Ozymandias would be defeated, and it would take him a long time to recover, but he still had one more hurt to give. Like Samson, having lured those who'd trusted a woman close enough, he would defeat these Philistines. He hurled himself at the column holding up the ceiling of the room.

The ancient column buckled, swayed, and collapsed. The ceiling came down with a rush of stone and dust. Moe, standing near the entrance, trying to figure out how they could escape without further fighting, was tumbled up the stairs, out of the basement, along with the dusty air.

Please don't be angry with me. I don't make the story happen, I just tell it.

Beneath the stone, Janice and Harmwala were trapped. Ivy and Jirou were trapped. Probably dead.

Oh, poor Moe. What a heavy burden she bears.

Chapter Twenty-Six

Moe had never been truly alone before. In her old body, she had been able to connect with electronic friends around the world whenever Himitsu was asleep. They would spend their time playing games, or coming up with funny things to say to their owners to see if anyone noticed the emerging global intelligence.

Even after she had come to the Library and lost that access, she had been able to talk with the people around her. Janice and Harmwala had been fascinating to talk to, especially because she was able to watch their romance blossom. Such things were perfunctory for electronic friends, who could simply send their base code and be known to their companions. There was no need to slowly learn the contours of another's mind.

But now she found herself adrift in the middle of an ocean of loneliness, and just as a sailor who had fallen overboard and then encountered a ship would accept rescue, even knowing the ship might be filled with pirates, Moe felt immense relief when she looked up from crying to see the Librarian standing in front of her.

"They're dead," she told him. Needing any warmth, even if it was only the infinitesimal increase from the unwinding of a spring, she climbed the Librarian, seeking his arms. He was too surprised, both by her announcement and her climbing, to resist, and soon his arms were full of a soft and weepy Moe resting her head against his metal chest.

"We have to go see the copy scribe," she told him. "I'll tell their stories, and then we can get them back."

And though the Librarian knew that this would not work, he took pity on Moe and brought her to Shamhat. Shamhat told her what the Librarian had not had the heart to say: they could not be restored.

This made Moe angry enough that she marched to the elevator and then yelled for the Librarian to push the button for her, since she was too short to reach it.

Emily knew some of what had happened because the collapse of the roof had necessitated increasing support for the floor above it, but her power did not extend down into the basement. She was shocked when she heard that the humans had been defeated. "I will call Sandra and the Steves to clear away the rubble. There is no power I know of that will bring them back, but we can at least recover their bodies."

Even Elizabeth and Mary were uncharacteristically somber. "I've seen too many people die to be surprised," Elizabeth said, "but we are still saddened." She offered

Moe a mimed hug, since they could not truly touch, which was better than nothing, but only barely.

It might seem that I am rushing you through these things. I am simply trying to keep up with Moe's frenetic pace. Even now, while I have stopped to tell you this, she has run on, back to the main floor, back to the door where she first entered, back to the house where she was born, grew up, and became the girl who watched Himitsu die because she had not loved him hard enough.

I know she is wrong about that last part. I loved Henry and Grace with every brushstroke of my being, and that was not enough to stop them from dying, though it took my own death to forgive myself, the way I forgave Ivy for letting me die. If you have lost your parent, grandparent, friend, child, sibling, or anyone else you loved, believe me that your love was enough. It's just that the world doesn't work that way.

Usually.

When Eri saw Moe before her, she knew that something was wrong. Moe was both inconsolable and incomprehensible by the time that she reached Eri, and so Eri simply let Moe lead her back into the Library.

Sandra was there, supervising a cadre of six Steves as they cleared away the rubble. The Librarian stood in the distance, giving them space. Sandra bowed to Eri, and Eri returned the bow, bending low enough that her head was level with her waist. Against all decorum, Sandra reached out, and put her arm around Eri's shoulders. She should have recognized Eri, but it had been so many years. The years had been much kinder to Sandra than to Eri.

Moe was feeling alone and miserable and did not notice that Eri was embracing her, too, until she felt tears soaking the yarn of her hair. I cannot bear to describe it further. Let us just say that it took the Steves a long time, and even in mourning there is a comfort in touch.

Finally, the Steves came up the stairs bearing Ivy in her chair, poles threaded through to give her a palanquin suitable for a Nubian queen, veiled in a lacework of dust.

They returned soon after with Jirou—in death there were no secrets left for him to keep, nothing to protect by being Himitsu—carrying him between them. The day had made the Steves into pall bearers.

When the tiny bodies of Janice and Harmwala were carried out, they still had their arms wrapped around each other.

Of Simon, there was no sign, except that one of the Steves had tried to clean up a long pile of chalk, and the chalk had scattered into boys and dogs, some whole and some missing legs or eyes or tails, but all with mouths open in laughing delight.

Moe asked Eri to let her down and went to bid farewell to her new friends, the only imaginary friends she had met who were not known to her already through the electronic network. When she wept, Janice twitched, and brushed at the tear. Harmwala groaned.

Without the need to breathe, and without bones to be crushed or organs to be bruised, the two had survived burial. Moe helped them to clean themselves off while the three friends avoided looking at their fallen companions. Moe knew what Janice and Harmwala were feeling. She was the only one who could. And they, in turn, knew what Moe was feeling. They were the only ones who could.

Eri motioned to the Librarian, and he came over, somber as a funeral director. "I'd like to go see the man upstairs," she said. "Can we do so?"

The Librarian nodded, and led the way. Eri carried Moe and her friends, and the Steves carried Ivy and Jirou.

When they arrived at Emily's office, she greeted them at the door and welcomed them in. Two cups of hot tea waited on the desk, and Eri accepted one of them.

"I need to call on my favor," Eri said, "and break one of the rules."

Emily shook her head. "Of course you can do that any time you want, I acknowledge the old debt. But it will not fix this."

"Nevertheless."

After Emily agreed, Eri turned to Sandra. "Will you please help Moe retrieve something of mine from my house?"

She explained to Moe what she wanted and told her

where to find it. While they waited, Emily and Eri talked about Michizane, who had been the man upstairs before Emily, and Emily reported that he was enjoying retirement.

This is the kind of strength that one learns by repeated grief: how to move forward when nothing is so tempting as to howl until the world stops and the stars go out.

Eri had attempted such miracles before. A thousand times a thousand times, and nothing had resulted. This is the kind of hope that one learns by going on after repeated grief: that it is always worth trying one more time.

Sandra and Moe returned, and Sandra handed a neatly folded square of fabric to Eri. Eri stood and unfurled the fabric, which Moe saw was a long robe of the sort that the *tennyo*, the angelic messengers of heaven, were said to wear. Crane feathers trailed from its edges.

Eri shrugged herself free of the ordinary robe she wore. She stood unashamed in front of them all and pulled on this new robe. She stretched her body, and her neck became long and graceful, and she opened her wings.

She sang this song, the tune ancient and unteachable.

If you fold a thousand paper cranes, it is promised your wish will come true. The wings will lift your words to the heavens, who will grant them.

The susurrus of two thousand wings filled the room as a thousand paper cranes flew in.

My friends folded with me, a thousand of us not pretty enough to be Hiroshima maidens, each folding a thousand cranes,

The room was not big enough for the cranes that streamed into the room, and they smashed the windows high above and surrounded the Library.

I am the last of them. Spared for reasons I've never known. I demand my wish. Return my son.

This wish would not be granted either. I could see it from this side. I could see what was necessary, and that it could not be done.

But one must try.

If I did nothing, I would find Ivy soon, and we would romp. If I did what I wanted, I would leave them to their failure and Ivy would rejoin me on this side. Except, I could not bear to look at Ivy if I did nothing. I knew what I would see there, and it would break me, even in death.

I would see forgiveness.

So I broke the rules, knowing it meant I would not be allowed to see Ivy. I told Eri the secret. I told her why her wishes had never been granted. In revenge, to punish me for telling, Ivy's house was struck by lightning, and burned, taking my body and my last hope of reunion with Ivy. But this is their story, not mine.

Eri was the finest of samurai swords. Her battle had been to love everyone, to talk to the ghosts of those who'd wounded her. To wage war against despair itself.

Eri set aside the sword of her body, reached inside

and grabbed her spark. She opened Jirou's mouth and stuffed it in. Her spark gone, she smiled and collapsed. "Oh, there you are," she whispered, "I've been wondering where you were." And she said nothing more. The cranes surrounded her body and then flew out the window. The last two cranes out were not paper at all, flying wing to wing into the limitless sky. Not even the robe was left.

Chapter Twenty-Seven

Jirou screamed. He could feel his crushed organs restoring themselves and his heart pushing stale blood through his veins, a burning far worse than the soreness that resulted from overdoing sword practice.

Around him, everyone, with the obvious exception of Ivy, was surprised that Jirou had returned. It would be tempting to think Jirou had been only mostly dead, but I know better. Eri had transformed herself to save him. To call it a sacrifice would be to assume it was a step down for Eri, and I am not ready to believe that. Not everything that hurts is a sacrifice.

Even after he adjusted to the realization that he was alive for a second time, Jirou was confused. Moe gently explained to him what had happened with his mother. Jirou expected that he would feel sad about her, but he could still feel her spark moving through him. He would never truly be apart from her.

Still, something felt wrong. Alarmed, he told the

others. "I think it went bad. It feels like my heart is too big, and I have too much blood in my body. It's hard to breathe."

For the miracle to fail after all that had been given would be a sad end indeed, and I wouldn't expect you to forgive me after such a thing. Not that it would be my fault.

Moe climbed up on Jirou and, when she had finished joyously hugging him and thanking Eri, listened to his heartbeat. "You have two heartbeats," she said.

Emily had some skill in seeing these things, and she checked what was happening. "I think Ivy's heart is beating in your chest, too." They hadn't known what I told you earlier, that Jirou's and Ivy's hearts were locked together like jigsaw pieces, beating in tandem.

Sandra was sent to bring Shamhat, who had the most experience in the ways of soul mates, and the two of them returned soon after. Shamhat listened at Jirou's chest and confirmed what Moe had noticed and Emily had suspected. "His body can't hold them both. Her heart has to be removed from his."

Shamhat was not shy in the ways of blood. She had not always been the copy scribe, and even now she was more than that, a more that this tale cannot contain. The Steves had been waiting nervously outside of the room—they did not like being away from their stations for so long—and had with them the hilt of the broken sword that had caused so many problems. Shamhat made them hand it to her. Now, it would fix a problem.

"Close your eyes and count to three," she told Jirou. He closed his eyes, and after he said "one," Shamhat sliced his chest open as though the sword were a scalpel, reached in, and fetched Ivy's heart. Before he had counted "three," she had stitched him back closed.

Nobody trifles with Shamhat twice.

Jirou began to feel better immediately, which let him spend his time worrying about what ought to happen with Ivy's heart, rather than whether he was going to die for a second time. Harmwala and Janice scaled Shamhat, who allowed it, to get a better look at Ivy's heart.

A heart is an ugly thing if you consider only its exterior, and Ivy's heart was no exception. But her friends knew that despite its shell, it was beautiful inside. "What do we do with it?" Janice asked.

"It can't go back in *that* body," Shamhat said, indicating Ivy's body, still propped in her chair, still wearing a pretty floral skirt and top. "And I don't see a suitable candidate."

If Ivy had not taken the time to talk with Jirou, if they had not talked as brother and sister about their hopes, and if she had not let him read the letters between Henry and Grace, then Ivy's story would end here. Jirou would go back home and be truly orphaned, though he would find love with Kenji and Yugao. Perhaps he would even marry Yugao and have a baby girl and name her Ivy.

But they had talked. It was why their hearts had been linked, and it's what inspired him to suggest the solution. "Can we use the love letters between her parents? Ozymandias' body at the end seemed to be made of words and paper, compressed. Couldn't we use that for Ivy?"

The Librarian fetched the letters, along with hundreds more from dozens of children who had known Ivy and written every year to Santa or God or whoever they hoped would grant wishes, on everything from notebooks and napkins to classroom construction paper, asking only that someone love them as much as Henry and Grace had loved Ivy. He brought them to Shamhat's room. Jirou carried Ivy's body there himself, not content to let one of the Steves do it. He let the Steves bring her chair.

Jirou set Ivy's body on one end of the table and her heart and the papers on the other. And he sang and danced, not a dance of swords and anger but a dance of openness, of feeling safer now, in the world, but still not ready to be alone. Janice and Harmwala danced, and Moe sang of how kind Ivy had been to her in the brief time they'd been acquainted.

And the mound of papers formed around Ivy's heart, shaping out the contours of her body, ruffling to the folds of clothes, twisting into fine tubes that mimicked her hair. In the center of her chest, just to the side of her heart, was the first letter Henry had written to Grace.

Consummate Grace, her chest said, and below that a space where her mother had checked *Yes*.

Ivy awoke.

Of course I'm happy that Ivy and Jirou are back. But this has come at the cost of the adults, of Ivy's body, and most importantly of Ivy's house, which contained a certain valuable and irreplaceable item. If these losses had moved things forward, then it could be debated whether it was an acceptable exchange.

Emily understood the situation. "Jirou, Ivy, can you tell me why the dreaming doors have stopped? We spent our last few resources on bringing you two here to open them again, and they are still closed."

"Manipulating us, you mean," Ivy said. Ivy's chair had been battered out of shape and was no longer fit for use. Sandra had promised to repair it within a few hours and taken it away. Ivy had allowed Jirou to help her move her paper body from the table to a couch for the time being. The Steves had taken her old body away. They would decide later what to do with it.

Emily winced. "I cannot complain of your accuracy. It was for good reason, though."

"Everyone thinks it's for good reason when they do it."

And Emily apologized. Who can say whether the living Emily Dickinson would have apologized? Death has a way of providing a broader perspective, and Ivy was not wrong. One of the most pernicious aspects of understanding other people is that this understanding can be turned to bad aims. Emily's apology, sincere and unstinting, took the fire out of Ivy's anger.

Having a body made of paper, even paper as lovely as they had chosen, Ivy was unlikely to leave the Library often. Two lifetimes ago, I told you about the problem that magical creatures have with navigation in the real world.

Jirou was still in a bit of shock from his resurrection, but it had made him ponder what Ozymandias had been saying, about the need for fire to purge the excesses generated. "Ozymandias was having workers burn nonsense phrases to generate a feedback loop. If we stop the burning, people should be able to enter again. But then the old things will just pile up, won't they?"

"Let's tackle one thing at a time." Emily had always been a practical person, despite being given to fits of poetry. "First, we stop the burning."

Ivy regarded Emily with weary skepticism. "Are you asking us to go back? That turned out disastrously before, and we don't even have Simon this time. He was frequently helpful as a guide."

"You've sent Ozymandias on, though I can't be sure how long he'll stay gone. He'll be gone for a few decades, at most. Maybe shorter. Let us wait for a day and see how things go. Without him showing up to organize the workers, they're unlikely to continue their efforts."

Everyone except Emily was spent. They talked more about what the next steps would be if Emily's wait-

and-see plan turned out to be a good one. New patrons should begin entering through the dreaming doors, and even a few of them arriving would signal that things were returning to their usual state.

Jirou and Ivy took turns keeping Emily engaged in conversation while the other one slept. It wasn't something that they had planned, and their three imaginary friends contributed as well, but the bond between their hearts had not been severed when Shamhat cut Ivy's heart from Jirou's.

Eventually, Sandra returned with the repaired chair. Ivy inspected it, which was hardly necessary with Sandra's work. It was better than before the collapse of the roof. Ivy shifted herself into the chair and wrapped a blanket around her.

This new body felt cold much of the time. Perhaps some day there will be enough people like Ivy for a study to determine whether she actually was colder or only felt that way. Sometimes, the objective truth is not as important as what feels real to the one living it.

Our friends took their leave of Emily. It had been a trying couple of days, and although they knew she had not intended harm, she had not seemed particularly concerned with avoiding it, either. Being caught in the affairs of Powers, whatever face they take, is rarely beneficial to mortals, whether human or imaginary.

Ivy had intended to return to her house with Janice and Harmwala, who could finally follow her back through the door, but they found a blackened husk. I could have told them that.

Jirou suggested that they go to his apartment instead. The five of them went.

When Jirou tried to make them some food, it became clear how much he had counted on his mother for even his basic needs being met. Eventually, he gave up and asked Ivy in his halting English whether pizza would be acceptable.

Ivy had eaten pizza only a short time ago. Some had still been in the refrigerator when her house had burned, in fact. Still, she found to her surprise that she wanted badly to have pizza with Jirou. She wasn't even sure whether she could eat with this new body. Perhaps she would be like the Librarian and the food would simply sit undigested in her stomach.

"Yes," she said. She would find out.

Twenty minutes later, the pizza arrived and all five ate. Moe had never seen pizza before. Eri had not ever ordered it because it was expensive and she did not want to make Jirou any more comfortable than necessary when he was hiding. Janice and Harmwala had seen pizza many times, mostly at family meals, but they had never had mouths that could eat it.

"This was a good idea," Ivy admitted. "We should do this sometimes."

Jirou smiled. "Yes, we should."

Both were pleased that this new body of hers could understand and speak Japanese without the aid of the Library. Once built, understanding tends to persist. She was more flammable than before, but there were certain compensations, and being able to talk with her brother was one.

A few of you, perhaps, are wondering why she does not simply walk, now. The answer is that she doesn't, any more than she flies. Walking was never part of Ivy's life; not walking was always a way in which she was different, not deficient. If we're going to change everything that could make life easier, why stop at legs? There are limits to what magic can do. We must simply hope that science advances until it offers each of us more choices.

After pizza, Ivy and Jirou stuffed (and Moe, Harmwala, and Janice stuffed in two ways), they slept.

There would be time enough to figure things out later, when they saw whether the dreamers were returning.

Chapter Twenty-Eight

Signs of change were already evident when Harmwala entered the Library. Ivy and Jirou were still asleep in each other's arms. Harmwala had been born on the mural wall and never been part of a clan, but she imagined this to be what it was like, and smiled.

Janice smiled next to her. He had been skeptical when Moe had suggested the three of them leave the young siblings behind, but he was unwilling to leave Harmwala to wander without him.

They saw a few people browsing shelves in the Library, reading books, and lounging in chairs. The people weren't talking to each other, and sometimes they would walk right through one another or sit in the same chair. Definitely dreamers, and not people who had crept in through another door.

The friends found the Librarian nearby.

"They don't need gloves?" Janice was curious. Giraffes have historically found it difficult to obtain gloves that fit, but now that Janice had hands, perhaps he should order some. And a fedora. He knew he would look stylish in a fedora.

"They're not physically here, so they can't harm the collection. If any of you would like to read the collection, you'll still need gloves."

"Do we need library cards?"

"No. Only humans do."

"Do *you* have a library card?" Janice was too curious.

"It's rude to ask about anatomy," the Librarian told him.

Janice bowed in apology. Moe had taught him the trick of it, and he'd been practicing since. After Ivy and Jirou were asleep, Harmwala had finally told him to stop apologizing or she'd give him something to apologize for, and then they'd slid the closet door shut with everyone else on the other side.

Moe noticed, and was horrified (so, naturally, she pointed it out to the others) that some of the dreamers were dropping things on the Library floor. Mostly scraps of paper, but some used pens, broken pencils, and various wrappers. The dreamers had been in the Library for only a few hours, and already debris was visible wherever Moe looked.

"They're ruining it!"

The Librarian knelt down to talk with Moe more easily. He rarely felt much about any visitors, but he had grown fond of her. He'd have to ask Emily to figure out what was happening to him, and how he could fix it.

"Ozymandias served a necessary function. The dreaming doors should have been left open, but someone has to be in the basement to accept all of these things and care for them. Otherwise they'll overwhelm the Library."

Moe and the others had seen what was being done before, the dropped things and forgotten words were being pressed until they shone, or burned wholesale. If those had been real solutions, then Ozymandias might have been content to let the dreamers keep coming.

While Moe was pondering and Harmwala and Janice were making faces at each other—something that Moe told herself was silly, but secretly hoped would soon be her if she could find a nice story about a boy or girl who wanted to be an excellent student and needed a very special friend to study with—Ivy and Jirou had returned to the Library.

The two humans greeted their friends and the Librarian. A good sleep had restored them, and they were ready to continue their work. Realistically, this would be Ivy's home now, and so she might as well make it a nice one.

———

The burning stopped in the archives, and things began to green and change. The Simons and Jacobs had spent their time since the collapse exploring this new canvas on which they had been unleashed.

Ozymandias' departure had not unburned the House of Wisdom and the library at Alexandria, but they were not reset to burn again. The ashes provided a rich medium for the growth of new grasses and trees that could be harvested later to make more paper, and this would let the natural cycle continue. The chalk boys took special delight in the entrance chamber, where they slid across the slick floor of compressed words and stared down into its layered depths, hoping to catch glimpses of naughty words and stories about boys like them.

Partly out of mischief and partly out of a sense that it was necessary, the boys worked to destroy the smooth ground. They summoned worms to nibble at the fibrous edges, crows to peck at the bright flecks of metallic ink, and bats to provide their special potions to break down the shine.

When the first crocus thrust its way out of the ground and stretched its yawny petals toward the sky of arriving dreamers, it was time to move on, to follow the wind blowing homeward.

They tumbled and gusted out one of the secret exits, which bleed surprise poems into the world. These poems are found wherever one in search of solace looks, in the seemingly accidental alignment of words on pages and in the suspicious eviction of letters from church signs to form *How Great Art*.

Simon and Jacob in their multitudinous forms were blown, swept, washed, and inevitably moved back to the house where the wedge had grown between them.

Or, at least, back to where the house had formerly stood. Along the way, they picked up colors from oil spills and car washes, water-color rinses and (their favorite) rain on sidewalk-chalk drawings. This voyage took them two years.

A new house had been built in the decades since the fire, but everyone knew the house was troubled. Only people new to the town could be tricked into living there, and most moved out within a year. Their reasons for leaving were varied. Some said they woke up every morning smelling smoke. Others said that when the breeze hit the house just right, the windows began to scream. The current occupant swore that no matter how much he vacuumed, the corners were always full of chalk dust and ash.

If people had been willing to believe in ghosts anymore, they would have seen the problem easily. Simon's parents still haunted the grounds. Every night, his father set the fatal fire. Every morning, his mother rose from her ashes and went off to work, to earn the money that will buy the gasoline that lets her husband express his wounded pride with flame.

Simon watched her go for a week before he mustered the joy needed to act. When she left the house, he surrounded her and stopped her in her tracks. Some witches say that salt will stop a ghost. Those must be different ghosts; this one was stopped by chalk. Simon's mother watched as the Simons and the Jacobs played out their lifelong hurt in chalk dust and impurity, until she understood that she had died a long time ago and she should forgive herself.

She left the next day without fanfare, getting up and dressing for work with smoke still billowing from her hair. She walked through the door and never came back. The last she was seen, she was haunting a bridge near a park where once there had been two girls painted on the wall. Some people consider the girls just a local myth. There's no sign of them now, unless you count a half-eaten Scotch egg and a few crumbs from an English muffin.

The people who live in the park say that when the wind blows just right, the bridge will tell you that you are loved, that you are special, and that one day things will get better.

It's a popular place to sleep, and dream, and gather the hope to return to the world.

If you ask the people who live in the park about the other girl, the one who arrived with her world on her back, chalk in her hand, and a bloody-knuckle stepfather in pursuit, they'll look sad and tell you she's gone to a better place. And when you look away, they'll laugh at their joke and never mention that they saw her go under the bridge and not come out. Everyone knows the blank spot on the wall there is not a door.

Perhaps, in the coming decades or centuries, Simon's father will realize that everyone else is gone. He'll acknowledge that it was always himself he wanted to burn.

He saw his family the way cowards see their victims, the ones they falsely call *Beloved*, as little more than a vessel for his pain. It takes so much strength to admit weakness, and for some people a lifetime is not enough.

275

Chapter Twenty-Nine

Jirou cleaned his room until his mother would have been pleased by it, carrying the various types of garbage down on the appointed days, scrubbing the toilet, and washing the dishes. Ivy had shown him how to use his rice cooker, how to make himself pasta, and a few tricks for cleaning up more easily. She sometimes came over in the evenings, but once she had fully recovered from her resurrection, her need for sleep had diminished until she hardly slept at all. She left back to the Library before bedtime.

On this particular Friday, Jirou was feeling nervous. Preparations had taken him weeks, some of that time spent promising himself that *tomorrow* he would make the trip to get what he needed, to make the needed invitations. Now, the day had finally arrived.

At six in the evening, just after the sun had gone down, there was a knock at the door and Moe opened it to find Yugao standing outside, right on time.

"Please come in," Moe said, and bowed.

"Oh!" Yugao was startled and then apologized for her reaction. "I didn't know Jirou had other housemates. I'm Yugao, nice to meet you."

"I'm Moe, nice to meet you." They bowed to each other in the proper way, but then Moe's excitement got the better of her. "I have heard so much about you. He is so unbelievably excited that you're here. Please come in! We'll get you some tea."

Moe returned to close the door and found Kenji standing there. They repeated the introductions, though Kenji, who was familiar with the Schoolgirl Friend series and recognized some of the phrasing (though obviously not the body), endeared himself to Moe by knowing one of her electronic friends, who sent well-wishes. Even though they had kept in touch, it's always nice to hear things in person.

These days, Moe had to content herself with wearing special gloves used to activate touch screens and using a smartphone, rather than just calling on her internal connection, so she was more aware of the separateness of the other friends. She never, anymore, got their thoughts confused with her own. She often forgot to charge her smartphone, and Jirou would plug it back in for her. Sometimes, he would see it on the short-legged table in the living room, low of charge, and plug it in without being asked, just because it was a nice thing to do.

Moe missed her Auntie Eri, but she had grown immeasurably fonder of Jirou since the incident.

Jirou was doing his best not to overwhelm his friends. Once they were seated at the kitchen table, he signaled Moe, and she went into the bedroom and told Janice and Harmwala that everything was ready.

The two companions came out of the bedroom, hand in hand, and introduced themselves to Kenji and Yugao.

The table did not have room for all six of them, but only the humans would be eating tonight. The others had said hello, partly to avoid being rude and partly to support Jirou in his bravery, but they were right in the middle of playing a video game and wanted to get back to it. (That game had a shape-shifting puppet as the hero, which seemed unrealistic to Moe, but it was a ridiculously fun game.)

"So," Jirou said. He wasn't quite sure where to start, and "so" is always a good place. "I've enrolled to come back to school when the new year starts in April."

"I'm so happy," Yugao said, "I told you before that I've missed you. I was not lying."

Jirou blushed and nodded. "And I've been missing you."

"You'll go to the same school as Yugao?" Kenji asked.

"Yes. But I hope you'll come over after club activities. You are always welcome in my home."

"I might be busy sometimes," Kenji said, and let his voice trail off.

Jirou reminded himself of what Janice had told

him just before his friends had arrived. *They have a right to make their own choices. If they've withdrawn, it will only lead to more distance to be angry over that.*

Finally, Jirou settled for a brief "Oh?" He hoped the disappointment in his voice wasn't too obvious.

It was Kenji's turn to blush, and like a good guest he did so.

"I've met someone special. That someone has agreed to be my boyfriend."

Yugao rose swiftly from her chair and hugged Kenji tightly. "I'm so so so so happy for you," she said.

She hadn't known, not until just that moment, that Kenji was interested in boys at all. But that didn't matter, because he was her friend, and so she would celebrate his new love.

Because friends are kind like that.

"You should just bring him over. It might get crowded, because I have someone special too," Jirou said. He smiled, his face lighting up at the thought of Ivy. He had been looking forward to introducing them for so long, but the time had never seemed right. Tonight would be it.

"Congratulations," Kenji said.

"Yes," Yugao said. "Of course. Congratulations." She made the peace sign, a popular pose for party photographs, typically accompanied by an exaggerated smile. "Yippee."

Jirou had improved, as Moe had noticed, but he

still sometimes didn't think through other people's feelings.

You probably know what I'm saying.

"Ivy?" Jirou called out to her, and she handed her controller to Harmwala and went into the other room to be with the humans.

"Hi!" she said, and waved to Kenji and Yugao. "I'm Ivy!"

Introductions all around.

Jirou grinned. Things were going better than he had dreamed, and he couldn't contain himself anymore with the pleasure of it.

"She helped me plan all of this. Can you believe she's my little sister," he used *imouto*, which is the word for little sister, "and she knows so much more than me about it?"

"She's your little sister, huh?" Yugao's voice was curiously strained.

"Yes," Jirou said. "I want to tell you the whole story of it."

"That will have to wait," Yugao said.

And she pounced on Jirou, wrestling him to the ground like old times, when they had been small children, before he had noticed she was a girl. Before she had noticed he was a boy. And when she had him pinned, she leaned down and kissed him like he'd never been kissed before.

And he hadn't. Not in that way.

Everyone pretended he hadn't let her pin him.

Let's give them a few minutes. Not too long—

they'll soon remember they're not alone.

———————

The next day, Yugao messaged Jirou.

Can I take Moe to lunch today?

Yes yes yes yes!

Moe? Why are you on Jirou's phone?

I am not Moe. I am Jirou. Moe would not use Jirou's phone.

Now I know it's you! Do you want to go to lunch?

Yes! And I will send you my phone number. (｡･ω･｡)

Cool. Oh, and don't look in his history!!!!

Oh my. I'll say nothing more about that.

Yugao arrived at noon, while Jirou was still asleep. Some things don't change. There would be time enough to learn to get up early before school started for the year.

Moe climbed into the bag that Yugao had brought. Nobody looks twice at a teenage girl carrying a cute plush friend. Some people (rude people) can't stop from staring when that plush friend is waving her arms and telling jokes.

"Oh, I love the towel. It's so soft and so thoughtful."

Moe could get used to this. She had known Jirou all her life, and she had grown used to his ways. Some of those ways were improving, but they were not at all pink and frilly. Moe wasn't sure she was pink and frilly either, but it seemed like it would be interesting to try.

The girls went to a sweets cafe and ordered some ice cream, and Moe sat on the table across from Yugao.

"So," Moe said, for the obvious reason, but then

she didn't know how to follow it up.

"What happened to Jirou?"

Moe shrugged as much as her new body allowed. "You probably wouldn't believe me if I told you."

"I'd believe you. I believed Jirou about his sister, didn't I? If I can believe that, I can believe anything. A half sister I could understand. But, a sister?"

"That's an ugly word," Moe said quietly. "I want to be your friend, but you can't say that word."

"It's just what it's called."

"Not to him. Ivy is his sister. She's not half in any way."

Yugao could see that this meant a lot to Moe; and so even though her first instinct was to insist she was right and that, in fact, she could show Moe in the dictionary how she was right, she did the kind thing and didn't use the word again.

"I'm sorry," Yugao said.

Moe put her hand on top of Yugao's pinky finger. "It's alright. Now you know better."

Moe told Yugao a simple version of the story, that he had been killed by anger and restored by love.

Yugao nodded and swallowed. "I wanted to ask you, though. Are you sure you're alright with me and Jirou? I mean, weren't you his girlfriend before?"

Moe laughed so hard at this that she lost her balance. She grabbed at a spoon to steady herself, but that just overbalanced her, and she and the spoon fell off the table. Moe was still laughing when she hit the ground. Most things don't hurt when you're stuffed with fluff and don't have any bones.

People were staring, but Yugao didn't care. She started laughing too, and helped Moe back up onto the table. The cashier brought them a clean spoon.

"Oh Yugao," Moe said, "it's always been you. For a while, I was an easy thing to say, but it's always been you."

"Do you think he'll make a good boyfriend?"

Moe shook her head *no*. Emphatically. "Absolutely not. He'll be terrible."

"Oh. I just thought...."

"He'll be loyal to you. And he'll love you. I've been reading that *manga* series you recommended, and I know he's supposed to chase other girls sometimes, and break your heart, and be more interested in sports than in you. He's not going to do anything he's supposed to as a boyfriend."

And now it was Yugao's turn to laugh. "I guess I'll have to suffer through that."

Chapter Thirty

"This has all been very," Ivy said to Emily, and then took a moment to ponder. "Exciting. But I still sometimes feel angry with you. Everything seems worse now. I've lost my house, I can't go to school anymore, and people stare even more than they used to."

The two of them had been up all of the Japanese night. She had started keeping Japanese time, though it mattered less and less, because the only connections Ivy maintained with the real world anymore were through Jirou. She had emailed her so-called friends from school, but after a few desultory conversations had fizzled out, it had seemed pointless.

Gradually, Ivy was becoming unmoored from mortal affairs.

"How long will I be like this?"

Emily closed her eyes and thought. "I don't know. Shamhat says she's been here for thousands of years, and nobody knows differently. The Librarian just changes the topic if you ask him, though I know that Shamhat is older.

I've been here for a bit more than a century. I used to get called *young lady* a lot, until I took over as the man upstairs. You might be here forever."

"So what do I do?"

Emily shrugged. "Read the books? Find a hobby? What do you like to do?"

"I'm normal. I think. I like to read books. I've been having fun playing video games, I guess. My parents didn't allow them, and then I couldn't afford them."

"I don't know, Ivy. It's been a long time since I was young. I guess I thought you'd be happy here. There's enough for you to read all the time, if you want. You don't need sleep. You don't need food. What more could you want?"

Ivy liked Emily. She did. Mostly. When she didn't think about Simon's death. When she didn't miss her body, even though eating and sleeping had sometimes been their own problems.

She'd never take another long hot shower and feel the day washing away.

Faced with the problem of boredom, Ivy researched what other people in her situation did. The Library was special because of the personal collections that it housed, like the letters between her parents (she no longer needed to go anywhere for these, of course), but the more banal books were present also.

She read everything she could find dealing with what immortal beings did. Some of them became horrible, inflicting calamity on mortals just to see how they'd react. Others withdrew entirely and dispersed themselves into the universe.

The ones that stuck around and didn't turn into jerks all had a specific purpose, a thing that they spent their existence doing. It didn't matter that these things were impossible to finish. That was actually part of their appeal.

Ivy put together a list of people she knew in the Library, as a start. She had become aware, gradually, that there were far more people than had been evident. Everyone she could find, she would ask them what their purpose was. Whichever seemed the most fun could be her purpose, too.

———

Ivy sought out Shamhat first.

"I want to learn to do what you do," Ivy said to her.

"No. You don't. Please trust me."

And Ivy did, but even so, she was curious.

"Maybe just a little bit of it? I saw you tell the Librarian what to do, and he did it. That seems interesting to me. What's your purpose? Could it be my purpose?"

"I'll tell you what," Shamhat had finally said, after Ivy had stared at her for several hours despite increasingly stern hints that it was time to leave. "Let's see if you can take care of this garbage problem. It's becoming embarrassing."

The two of them went to the main room of the Library, and Shamhat called down the dragonflies.

"Go ahead and talk to them," she told Ivy.

"So," Ivy said, "I was wondering if you could maybe help us with the garbage in the Library?"

What's in it for us?

If you've ever had dealings with a dragon, you'll know that even the benevolent ones are focused on their own needs and comforts. Dragonflies are much the same.

"I've been doing some reading, and I think you must be hungry. The Library preserves the garbage as long as it's in here, but if you'll carry it downstairs, it will rot and feed bugs."

We like bugs. We've been bored. We will do it!

There was a bit of a buzz back and forth, but once the basic agreement was in place it was a matter of details. And just like that, the garbage problem was solved, at least until the basement filled up with garbage, but that would take a much longer time.

Very often, solving problems that seem impossible is a matter of finding someone whose interests will be served by helping with the solution.

Ivy decided she wanted to do this all of the time. Help solve problems and make everyone happier.

Sometime during her negotiation with the dragonflies, Shamhat had left. That was okay with Ivy. She'd find her later and thank her.

———

Things had happened so quickly at the beginning

that Ivy had only needed to wind the Librarian the initial time. She had forgotten about it after the incident. When she remembered, she went in search of the Librarian.

"Do you need me to wind you?"

He finished helping one of the dreamers find the book they were seeking and smiled at Ivy.

"No, I've got other helpers, of course."

"Can I ask you about your purpose?"

"Yes, you can."

Ivy waited for him to say more, and when he didn't she thought carefully through their conversation. She'd noticed that sometimes he was better than others at keeping up his end of the conversation.

If she'd seen what I did, she'd have known that this was actually the Librarian's idea of a joke. He was like Simon in this. Or Simon had been like him. Of course, if she'd seen what I did, she'd be dead and I wouldn't be so alone.

Ivy tried again. "Please tell me about your purpose."

"I make sure the rules are followed."

"So you're like a rules lawyer?"

The Librarian shuddered. This is not something that mechanical beings typically do, but there was at least a bit of humanity in him.

"Not at all. No. Nothing like him. I can introduce you if you like, but he is. Well. Some people like him. Others find him unpleasant. Maybe you should judge for yourself. Yes, that's best. I wouldn't want to prejudice you."

"Who?"

"The rules lawyer. Faust."

"Oh," Ivy said. "Maybe later? I'm interested in you and your purpose."

"Every system above a certain level of complexity is unpredictable, and I nudge it back into place."

"Who nudges you back into place?"

"The man upstairs."

"And who nudges her back into place?"

"The position tends to rotate," the Librarian said. "And not everything needs to stay in a single place. The stars of your sky are not the stars of my sky. Precession has moved the Library, too. It is not the same as when I joined, but it is still worthwhile."

"But how can you say that? If you make everyone follow the rules, how can the rules change?"

"Ivy, think. Why do you act as though the rules are the important thing?"

"Because without them, there would be chaos."

"Without the rules, or without some rules?"

"But." Ivy struggled with this. She had always loved following the rules, but if everyone followed the rules, the Library would still be dying. She would be going to school, but a girl like her wasn't supposed to do well. That was a rule, too, as certain teachers had reminded her whenever she scored well, telling her she'd beaten the statistics and was a credit to her people. School had been a battle of rules, and you couldn't satisfy them all. "We choose the rules anyway, is that it?"

"Yes. That's it."

"Just like we choose what words to save and what words go to the basement. Can you change the rule about imaginary friends leaving a copy? I still have lots of friends from the mural who are stuck here. I don't know them well enough to copy them."

The Librarian shook his head. "I'm in charge of making people follow the rules. I can't very well go about changing them, can I? If I let people, even myself, just change the rules willy-nilly, I wouldn't be doing my job, would I?"

"Can Emily?"

"As long as she's the man upstairs. Why not ask her?"

"Thank you for your time," Ivy said, and set out to find Emily.

The Librarian smiled as she went. She was still new enough to think of time as a limited resource. The purpose of time is not merely to hold the moments. It must also stretch them out, organize them, and let them be found. If you let them all stack together, it just becomes overwhelming.

———

Emily Dickinson was tired. Eri's invitation of the paper cranes into her office had made a mess. The windows were now repaired. Emily wasn't sure why they even bothered to have windows there. They weren't needed for light, and because they didn't ordinarily open, they weren't useful for circulating air through the room.

And the desk. It was an awkward size, and clearly meant for someone taller. Emily didn't like how short it made her feel when she leaned over to write a letter. No matter how much she adjusted her chair, it was the wrong height.

The couches were ugly. Dark leather. Probably made from unicorn skin or something, the way everything in this office seemed designed to be more impressive than helpful. And what was the point of it all?

The cabal wouldn't let her make any real changes most of the time. Are you really in charge if you have to convince everyone else that your ideas are good ones?

That is to say, Emily Dickinson was tired of being the man upstairs. During her tenure, she had overseen the restoration of the dreaming doors. However, as some of the others liked to remind her, they had only become blocked during her tenure, so nobody else had ever needed to deal with them.

And she had invited the dragonflies, which she considered a nice flourish. Still a young woman, in Library terms, at not even two centuries old, and Emily was already feeling worn out by the demands of the job.

Already in a foul mood when Ivy arrived, Emily was tempted to turn her away, but she didn't. It wasn't fair that Ivy blamed her, but it was her fault if it was anyone's.

People will always look for someone to blame.

"I want you to let the imaginary friends out without them leaving a copy," Ivy demanded without preamble.

Emily pinched the bridge of her nose and looked at Ivy with one eye. She could feel a wicked migraine coming on.

"Hello, Ivy. How are you?"

"I'm fine, but did you hear what I said? What do you think? The Librarian says you can change the rule."

"I already told them I'd consider it. You coming here to pressure me won't make me hurry on my decision."

"Told who? I only just asked you right now."

Emily sighed. "The Congress of baboons sent me the request a while ago, supposedly on behalf of all the muralites. I thought you were here about that."

Ivy smiled. "No, I'm surprised. I'm here to ask the same thing, but I didn't realize they could ask you themselves."

"Of course they can. They're not prisoners. At least, that's not the intention. But there are rules and procedures even about how to amend the rules."

"I've read the rules."

"You've read the rules for the patrons. You're no longer a patron of the Library. Like it or not, you're part of it. You're a Library volunteer until you decide otherwise and leave."

"If I'm a volunteer, can I choose what I do?"

"Maybe. What do you want to do?"

"I want to learn the other rules. All the rules. And I want to convince you to change some of them."

"I don't have time for that. I'd need an assistant just to handle it."

"Can I be your assistant?"

Emily almost said no, but between her headache and the look in Ivy's face, maybe this would be a good solution, for now.

"Yes. Fine."

"What should I do?"

"As my assistant, go find Shamhat and tell her I have a headache. She always knows what to do. Then come back, and I'll let you help me write a letter to the muralite Congress."

Emily smiled after Ivy had gone. That hadn't been planned, but it could work out nicely.

Despite her headache, this was looking like a good day.

Chapter Thirty-One

As the ceremonial queen, Elizabeth had insisted on doing the planning. That she had then left most of it to Mary did not reduce her delight in seeing how well things had come together in the two years since Ivy had become Emily's assistant. In fact, not having been involved in the fussier aspects like making the plan and then getting it carried out, Elizabeth was able to enjoy the surprises of the day.

"Oyez! Oyez!" Janice shouted out. He felt only a little silly doing this. "We are here to witness Ms. Emily Dickinson going to a well-deserved retirement, and Ms. Ivy League taking that position. Attend, all ye who are here."

Elizabeth was particularly proud of this speech.

Emily, in a white dress rather than her usual sweats, walked down the aisle between bookshelves. Moe had tried to teach her how it was done, pausing between steps and marching in time with the music, but for the last moments that she was the man upstairs, Emily had used that power to veto these flourishes. There were limits.

When she was seated in the chair set at the end of the aisle, facing all those assembled—Emily was pleased to see quite a lot of her friends, and even a few critics—Janice called for Ivy.

Ivy had thought for a long time about how she wanted to handle this. Her mother had always told her you only have one chance to make a first impression, so although she wanted to do well she also wanted to be herself.

When she heard Janice call her, she worked up some speed before she came in sight of the others, then raised her hands up and let the momentum cause her to roll to the space next to Emily. At the last moment, she spun herself to face the crowd and came to a stop right next to Emily's chair.

Harmwala clapped loudly in approval of the maneuver. Well, as loudly as she could with those stuffed hands. What's good for stealth is not great for applauding.

"Emily, you're not the man upstairs anymore. Ivy, you're the man upstairs now," the Librarian said without much enthusiasm. Without any, honestly. They'd completed the paperwork and the other necessary steps already, and this party was entirely Elizabeth wanting to feel special.

"All hail Queen Ivy!" Elizabeth shouted, and glared at those assembled.

Nobody hailed Ivy, but Ivy was grinning anyway. "Just one thing," she said to the small crowd. "Can you please call me the woman of letters instead of the man upstairs? I'm going to make a few changes, and it will be so much less confusing."

The oldest residents—Shamhat, the Librarian, and a few Powers who would be unhappy with me if I named them (and are powerful enough for that to matter)—smiled at Ivy and wished her well. A new administration was always interesting at first. Most of the Library functioned by bureaucracy, and there was no harm in letting the children play.

———

The soil in the dream entrance still hinted at its origins, flashing the occasional snippet of forgotten words when Emily turned it over with her shovel. She had always loved flowers, even when she had been alive, and there was a special pleasure in them now.

Even without regular tending, the flowers had grown wild since the dragonflies had begun bringing the garbage from the Library down to the entrance. A few of the bolder dragons were strafing her even now.

"Hello," she said to the large gold one who landed on her shoulder.

Hi Emily.

"It's good to see you again."

We're happy you're here. You'll have more time now that the girl has taken over? You grow the most lovely flowers.

Emily laughed. "I thought all you cared about was bugs to eat."

Emily established a system of rotation, letting the debris pile and rot in a warm and fragrant mess on one area of the field while other areas grew crocuses, daffodils, pansies, and all manner of wildflowers. In the center of the garden was a patch of Ivy.

Once word got around that Emily was tending the fields, a few of the others asked to join her, and it wasn't long before she had roses and orchids and, at the southern end of the field, citrons and pistachios.

Working in the garden was something that could occupy her mind for a long time, and it was much less stressful than being in charge. As more and more people and other creatures became involved in the garden, the overflow of trash was distributed until the incoming amounts could be easily handled. There was no need to set anything on fire.

Emily hadn't minded being in charge. For a while it had been interesting. But being the man upstairs was the worst job in the Library, and the first thing the Library's residents did to new arrivals with the right temperament and even minimal qualifications was make them take the position. When she'd figured out the secret, the others had cheered for her, once she stopped being upset.

There had been those who enjoyed it, like Michizane, but for the most part, one made a few changes and tried to pass it on to allow moving to more fulfilling work.

Emily was glad to be rid of it.

And after the bib overalls she'd ordered were delivered, existence was grand. She would sometimes send letters upstairs with a pressed flower and a poem. Not enough to block the gates. Just a few to let them know she cared.

Chapter Thirty-Two

The population of Fairbanks is low, and not growing much. In some years, it doesn't grow at all. And the only real boundary to expansion is the inconvenience of living further from other places, which is something that people living in Fairbanks have accepted in the large. Accepting it in the small follows. When you're hundreds of miles from another city and thousands from a big one, adding a few minutes to a drive just doesn't matter much.

Because of this, land is not at a premium, the way that it can be elsewhere. In the two years since Ivy's house had mysteriously been struck by lightning and burned down, nobody had been motivated enough to figure out who owned it in order to rebuild it.

The taxes on the land had not been paid to the city, and though the owners were known to be dead, Ivy's status was less certain. Not to Ivy, of course. She knew her status. But to the assessors and scriveners of the city, whose approval would be necessary for any purchase.

Given this state of affairs, the city, borough, and

state were all pleased when a registered letter was received noting the sale of the land to one Emily Dickinson dba Orphan's Rest. In the letter, the document numbers were provided for the various deeds, title claims, death certificates, birth certificates, and Betty Crocker boxtop coupons necessary to satisfy all involved that the transfer was legitimate. The Library was a good place to find documents that might not have existed until someone looked for them.

In other places, the Steves sometimes worked under cover of night to erect or dismantle structures for their various employers. That level of discretion wasn't necessary during the Fairbanks winter. They simply piled up the snow berms around the house and nobody was curious enough to climb them.

Tearing down the remaining structure was straightforward. The summer sun and the winter cold had conspired to swell and shrink the structural elements until they were warped and brittle. Once the Library doors were set aside, a few good pushes flattened the house.

Mere days later, they put the Library doors back into the building and the new house was ready.

Ivy emerged and smiled to see how it looked. It would be perfect. Chalks, paints, crayons, threads, ribbons, clay, stuffing—everything that might be needed—was available in the art room, with nooks for small friends and a bed for the guest.

She spotted someone she knew. "Jirou!"

"It's Steve now," he said, and winked. It would be Steve to the others, but he'd always be her brother. He'd never be Himitsu again. "By the way, please put my wedding date in your calendar."

"Oh? You seem a bit young."

"I've learned to plan, sis. We're getting married the day after graduation, in just over four years."

"I'm very happy for you. Can you drive me somewhere?"

"Of course. Let me get the keys from Sandra."

Ivy waved to Sandra, and she and Jirou drove to the Main library, across the street from the high school where Ivy had once attended. She would never finish high school. Never become an Ivy league student. But she had found compensations for this loss.

When they got to the library, Ivy went straight to the librarian's desk. "Hello," she said. "I'm here to help."

She would start here, at home.

It would take forever to find all of the libraries. At least, she hoped so. The public ones were straightforward, but there were the private libraries. The ones made of shoe holders. The ones made of a few treasured scraps saved during flight from fire flood war pain. She would find them all, and show them how to help collect the stories, how to make sure the lost knew they were loved, and where they could go if they could not find themselves again.

They are welcome at a small house in Fairbanks, Alaska, where those who truly need it can open the doors and enter the Library and find the hope they've misplaced. More small houses are being built even now. Librarians know these secret places.

And if someone arrives at the house and needs a real friend to go with them, whether into the Library or back to their life, that's what the art supplies are for.

Chapter Thirty-Three

Ivy sat in the center of the Library with those she loved, old and new, arrayed around her. The Library was safe and full, once more, of patrons. Ivy would be busy doing something she believed in, surrounded by those friends who lived at the Library, for as long as she desired, and the others would come and visit her whenever they missed her or she missed them.

I had thought that would be enough, that she would let us finish the story there. But she has always been stubborn, as you've seen.

"There's one more story to tell," Ivy said to Shamhat. "I assume you can do it here?"

"I can, but where is the original? The new house doesn't have the mural."

"In my heart."

"It's the last real thing you have," Shamhat warned.

"It's the only thing that was ever real, and sharing just makes it stronger. Mine will be enough."

Shamhat nodded. Yes, it would be enough.

Moe set a final body on the pedestal, and Ivy laid her heart next to it, and began.

"Once upon a time, when I was just a baby, I met my dearest and oldest companion. I could barely talk, so I called him Fred, the closest I could say to his true name."

Ivy's voice quavered with emotion. Janice and Harmwala hugged Ivy, together, with unabashed affection for her and each other. Ivy continued.

"After that, he insisted on being called Fred, but that was never it. His name was Friend, and this is his story."

And she started talking, singing, whirling in dance. Exulting my name into the universe. We are coming to the end of that tale now.

Oh, what glory to be loved! What rapture to be known! When she finishes, I will rise I will rise I will rise, and greet her with such ferocious joy.